WINTER'S RECKONING

A SEASONS OF MAGIC URBAN FANTASY NOVEL

SARAH BIGLOW

For information contact; www.sarah-biglow.com

Editing by: Under Wraps Publishing Services

Cover Design by: Deranged Doctor Design

ISBN: 978-1-955988-94-0

Published by Sarah Biglow: 2020

10 9 8 7 6 5 4 3 2 1

 Formatted with Vellum

SPECIAL THANKS

This edition was made possible by the support of so many wonderful backers on Kickstarter.

But I wanted to say a special thank you to **Myrdd, Clair John, Bill Lisse, Joe G., Jay A. Reynolds, Beth Wrege, Gerald P. McDaniel, Kandi, Lav, Kaitlyn, Cynthia Coffman, Kevin S. Varner, Jeffrey Tristan Thyme, Deborah Hedges, Stacy Shuda, Ryan Scott James, Mothy, Meredith, Seamus Sands and Tommy** for helping the campaign and these books soar higher than I ever imagined possible.

DECEMBER 18, 2017

ONE

Time has a weird way of speeding up and slowing down all at once when you're grieving. It had been eighty-nine days since a sniper—I believe it was an Order member—took Desmond from us. It felt like an eternity and no time at all had passed. In all that time he'd never come out of the pendant to explain himself—not once.

My heart skipped a beat every time I walked into the precinct. My mind liked trying to trick me into thinking that I'd see him again. He would be sitting in his office waiting for me or some other officer who needed help. However, the only time I saw his face there anymore was on the wall of fallen officers. He hadn't carried a badge and gun like the rest of us, but Captain Beech had lobbied for him to get a photo on the wall.

"I'm going to solve this, Des," I whispered to his photo as I stood in the hall. I could feel eyes on me as I addressed his portrait. I pivoted slowly to find Captain Beech standing behind me.

"I don't mean to interrupt," she said in an uncharacteristically soft tone. "But do you have a minute, Trenton?"

"Yes, ma'am," I answered. The words felt almost robotic as I followed her through the bullpen and into her office.

"Close the door," she instructed.

My palms grew sweaty as I eased the door shut and sat across from her. I could see a case file sitting on her desk with the label obscured. The captain folded her hands over the folder and said, "I wanted to check in with you. See how you're handling things."

"I'm fine," I replied

"Desmond was murdered right in front of you, Ezri. I most definitely wouldn't be okay if I were you."

"He's not the first person I've lost," I answered, averting my gaze.

"I know you lost your mother when you were young."

"Really, Captain I'm fine. I've got Jacquie, my dad and fiancé that I can lean on and the best place for me to be is right here, doing my job. Like he'd want."

She leaned back in her chair and regarded me in silence. Once upon a time I would have shrunk under that gaze. I could still remember the feeling of having my badge and gun taken from me nine months ago in this very office. The tiny hairs on the back of my arms stood on end as nervous energy bubbled just below the surface. A hint of strawberry wafted up to my nose, signaling my magic was ready to lash out at whatever was coming for me. I clenched my teeth, forcing my power back into check.

"I appreciate your dedication to the job. That's why I called you in here." She uncovered the case file and turned it to reveal Desmond's name. "I'm afraid we've officially classified his case as a Cold Case."

"No ... Captain, you can't," I protested.

"I'm sorry Trenton. Without any leads to go on, we've hit a dead end."

"Have they reviewed the video footage from the bank?"

"You know they have," she answered.

"What about the bullet? They recovered it, right?"

"It doesn't match anything in the system. I'm sorry. Unless you have any new information that you haven't already shared with the detectives assigned to the case, I'm afraid it's out of my hands."

I opened my mouth to protest more, but closed it. I'd told the officers assigned to the case everything I could remember right after it happened. Even so that didn't mean I didn't have more information to give them. I hadn't gone combing through my memory of that day. Part of me wanted to believe it was too painful to relive. While another piece insisted that I didn't need to go that route, because Desmond would show up and fill me in on everything. That hadn't happened though. Maybe it was time to take a trip down memory lane.

"There's nothing else," I finally said and stood. "If that's all, ma'am, I should get back to work."

"Here, take this to the records room, would you?" She passed me the file and I held it tight. I could feel the bulge of a thumb drive inside.

"Sure thing."

I retreated to my desk and grabbed my jacket, pocketing the drive. I had a stop to make before it and the file ended up in records. Jacquie appeared carrying two coffees. "We have a case?" She asked as I breezed by her.

"I'll explain on the way," I answered.

The coffee fortified me for what I was planning. Jacquie eyed me in silence as she pulled onto Commonwealth, following the flow of traffic away from the city and toward Authority headquarters in Newton. Since Desmond's death, I'd been staying away from the Council, much to their thinly veiled annoyance. I'd insisted we bring new people onto the Council to fill the vacancies left by the Order's attacks and then I'd ghosted them. Logically I knew I was falling back into old habits, but what's said about old habits is true.

"So, what did Beech want?" Jacquie finally broke the silence.

"They're shunting Des' case to Cold."

"Damn, Ezri, I'm sorry." I catch the sideways look of sympathy she shoots me before switching lanes. "You know that they did all they could with the evidence they had."

I swallowed the lump in my throat as she pulled into the circular drive of headquarters, the tiny drive in my pocket weighing on me. "I may have borrowed some evidence," I replied and darted out of the car.

I paused long enough in the front hall to catch sight of Teddy Cox racing after some other kids, their laughter echoing off the walls. He may have lost his sister to the darkness, but I'd still managed to keep my word to Lola. I'd kept him safe and out of the Order's clutches. He turned, spotted me and gave a quick wave before disappearing again.

"You realize this is illegal?" Jacquie hissed as I marched up the stairs with the flash drive in my hand.

"Avery is a police tech consultant. I'm not going to just give it to her," I argued as I made my way through the Council meeting room and into the tech hub.

Avery sat at the computer flipping through something on her screen. I cleared my throat and knocked on the doorframe to announce myself. I had enough time to catch a glimpse of a tab on her browser with the word séance in the title. She spun to face me, pulling her headphones from her ears. I could see the red rims of her eyes from crying. I couldn't blame her.

"I've got a job for you," I said and handed the flash drive over.

Looking over her shoulder I caught a glimpse of the images flashing on her computer screen. Images of her and Desmond over the years, places I'd never known they'd gone. From the Aquarium to a Duck Boat tour and down by the Esplanade.

She caught me looking and her cheeks flushed. "I'm making a memorial video for him. I needed to do something just to help make myself feel better, and this seemed like a good thing. I figure, he'd like it and it chronicles our whole relationship."

"It's nice," I said.

She tapped a few keys on the keyboard and the pictures disappeared. She slid the flash drive into a port on her computer and pulled up the security camera footage. Avery's shoulders stiffened as she hit play. "Why would you give me this?"

She slammed the space bar to make the video pause and turned her back on it. I shoved my hands in my pockets. "Because I need your help, Avery. They're filing his case as a Cold Case."

"Can they just do that?" She gulped, her voice jumping an octave.

"With a lack of evidence or witnesses, they have to devote their resources to cases they can actually solve," Jacquie answered.

I hated that my partner was right. Which is why I was standing here, asking my cousin's widow to work her literal tech magic to find me something I'd missed. Something the mundane techs wouldn't have spotted. "I need to know if there's anything magical on the footage. Please, Avery. Help me get him justice."

"You were there. Haven't you already done your memory walk thing?" She quipped, tapping a few other keys to minimize another set of browsers I couldn't read.

"I ... No." Avery didn't know about my pendant and how it worked. Or at least how I suspected it worked given all of the dead relatives that had popped up to lend advice and their magic in the last nine months.

"But you're fine with me having to watch the man I love die?" She ground out.

The more I thought about it from her perspective, I could see and even justify her anger. It did seem cruel to make her watch his last moments. I carried that memory with me. It wasn't fair to make her witness it, too. "I'll ask one of the others to do it. I just need to know if there is any trace of magic picked up by the footage."

"No. This is Desmond. *My* Desmond. No one else is laying hands on this footage." She looked up and her gaze was sharp enough to cut. "But don't ask me to help you again. Not unless you've had to live with this pain." She balled her hands into fists and took a sharp intake of breath. "I still feel him when I'm at home, like he's there trying to reach out to me. I can't walk past our favorite coffee shop or listen to classical music without hating the people that took him away from me."

I stood there in silence, having no idea of how to respond to her. Thanking her seemed heartless, but I didn't want her to think I had plans to go combing through my memory of that day just to ensure she would help me again in the future.

"Don't focus on him. I know it's hard, but try to focus on the sights and sounds around him, in the rest of the video," Jacquie offered.

Avery's gaze flitted to my partner before settling back on me. "I'll text you if I find anything."

She swiveled in the chair, pulled the headphones up over her ears and tapped a few keys on the keyboard in front of her. She pulled the flash drive out of the computer port and held it out to me without looking up. That was our cue to leave. I pocketed the drive and Jacquie led the way out down to the first floor.

"You're going to go digging in your memory, aren't you?" She asked once we were back in the car.

"I can't not do it, Jacquie. And not just because of what Avery said. I've been avoiding it for months." I studied the file folder in my lap, conjuring an image of Des smiling at me. "I was hoping he'd show me the way, but he's been silent. It's time I take the reins on this thing. If the police can't get justice for him, I'm going to do it. No matter what."

"Careful, partner. That's vigilante talk right there. You put that badge on to serve and protect people. It isn't a license to go off the rails, because you're hurting."

I turned to face her, my fingers tightening around the file until I was sure I'd come away with a mess of paper cuts. "The Order did this. The timing of his death is too suspicious not to be their dirty work. I don't know, maybe they got pissed I stopped them from stealing magic, so they wanted to hurt me. Whatever the reason, I know they're why Desmond is dead. This isn't about me being a cop. This is about me being the Savior."

"That may be true, but you go poking around places you aren't supposed to, and the very non-magical police are going to come down on you ... and hard. Captain Beech likes you, but she's got a department to run and doesn't need rogue cops."

I sighed. "It would be a lot easier if I knew my partner had my back."

She arched a brow. "When did I ever say I didn't have your back?"

"I didn't exactly fill you in on the plan," I answered sheepishly.

"You mean the plan you're half-assing right now?"

Guilty. "So, I need to drop this off at records before the Captain finds out about our little detour. First though, I need to make one more stop. I need to pay a visit to an old friend at the morgue."

TWO

In some small way I'd been lucky to not have to pay the morgue a visit since my first case back in March. I hadn't seen Assistant Medical Examiner Tricia Karo in that long either. Still I felt bad about not reaching out to her since then. Besides, that road went both ways.

She sat at a lab table; eyes pressed close to a microscope when we entered. The doors gave a pneumatic hiss as they closed behind us.

"Just a second," she said without moving.

I took the time to get myself back in the mindset of being a cop instead of an emotional wreck clinging to my need for justice. I knew Tricia wouldn't narc on us for looking into Desmond's death even though the case was closed. Despite that I still worried she might refuse my request. I'd practically had to twist her arm to test the knife my mother had used to kill herself.

"How can I ... Ezri. Hey, long time," she said, spinning around in her chair.

"Yeah, it has been," I agreed and stepped up. Jacquie stayed put near the door.

"You working a new case?" Tricia eyed the folder tucked under my arm.

"Not exactly." I opened the file just enough for her to see Desmond's face from his department ID photo. "I just had some questions."

"You aren't the investigating officer. I can't talk to you about it," she said.

I grabbed her wrist to keep her from rolling away. The smell of berries tickled my nose as a little magic slipped out, willing her to stay put. "I just need to know if you left anything out of the official report. Was there anything off about the bullet?"

"Off? Like what?'

"Like inexplainable stone dust at murder scenes," I answered.

The color drained from her face. "Everything I found is in the report. I wish I could tell you differently, but there was nothing remarkable about the bullet. The gun hadn't been used in any other crimes according to analysis."

"Are you sure? Could you test it again? Maybe the killer has gotten bolder in the months since and it will have a match now."

Tricia shook her head. "It would have come up if anything new was logged into the system."

"Please, can you check just one more time?"

Tricia gave me a sad look, but nodded and turned to her computer. I exhaled, not realizing I'd been holding in a breath as she typed. I waited, watching the progress bar on the search through the ballistics database. My heart leapt into my throat as it came up with zero matches.

"I really am sorry. I know you were friends."

"Something like that," I murmured, and my left hand grazed the pendant hanging from around my neck. After we'd reconnected, Desmond and I had agreed to keep our familial connection, far flung as it was, quiet. "Thanks for trying."

Jacquie gave Tricia a wordless nod as we retreated back to the car. "Now what?" She prompted.

"Now, I need to go for a little stroll down memory lane."

"Your fiancé is going to be pissed as hell at you for that."

"Only if he finds out," I reminded her as she put the car in drive.

The trees rose up along the street, their branches barren and forlorn as we made the trek to the condo J.T. and I had shared since September. It had finally started to feel like home. I wasn't eager to go diving back into my own trauma. Also, Jacquie was right, J.T. would be mad at me for doing it without any magical back-up. I didn't always emerge from these trips unscathed.

Sitting in the middle of the living room of my condo, watching Jacquie pace did nothing to help my nerves.

"You really should call him," she said, finally planting her feet.

"J.T.'s on shift right now. And it's not like someone else is going to try attacking me. It's my own memory. I'm safe."

I needed her to believe my words, because my track record for going into memories without ending up injured or worn out wasn't great. Except this time, I had no choice. If Desmond wasn't going to come out to play, I'd just have to go in and dig around myself.

"Maybe I should go with you. Two pairs of eyes are better than one," Jacquie offered.

"I appreciate the back-up, but I'm looking for signs of magic. And as kickass as you are, that's not really something you'll be able to help with."

"Just be careful."

I settled onto the couch and closed my eyes. "Can't make any promises."

My magic snapped to attention around me as I began to feed it my intent and desire. It built up around me like a bubble, encasing me within its protection.

The condo and Jacquie faded away, replaced by the bright autumn sunshine of a late September day. The hustle and bustle of the city rose up around me with the shadow of the bank looming behind. I stood a few paces away from the memory version of myself and Desmond. Swallowing the lump of fear in my throat, I let the memory play out.

The crack of the sniper rifle echoed in my ears as Desmond fell to the ground. I stood immobile as Memory Me went to him, calling for help that wouldn't be able to save him. I watched in horror as his magic latched on to me, binding us tight until it faded into the pendant. On instinct, I pressed my hand to the pendant. Nothing happened, but I didn't expect anything would either.

"Time to slow things down," I told no one in particular.

Before my eyes, the memory rewound and slowed to a frame by frame progression. I wanted to fast forward past the point where Desmond hit the ground, but I needed more information. So, I forced myself to walk forward and move around to Desmond's other side. I caught the bright light of the muzzle flash from a rooftop high above me. There'd been nothing to find up there, despite officers searching for clues. The sniper had been a professional.

This time, I waited for the bullet to appear in front of me and with a little bit of will, it stopped before striking Desmond. I plucked it from the air and studied it. The fact it felt warm against my fingers seemed odd. I suppose it made sense since being fired from a gun would cause friction and heat. Only it felt almost as if the heat was rippling from within the bullet, not just on the exterior.

Without losing control of the memory, I focused all of my senses on the bullet, the way the metal felt against the pads of my fingers. The weight of it and the smell of it. I expected the scent of gunpowder to waft from its surface, but that smell was overpowered by another, nauseatingly familiar scent. It stank of Reuben Wickham's magical signature.

"Got you now, you son of a bitch."

I tossed the bullet on the ground, grinding it out of existence. I knew it wouldn't change the memory. It wouldn't save Desmond's life, but it made me feel just a little better. I turned my attention to the origin of the shot. All the magic in the world couldn't reveal the identity of the shooter from this distance. I'd been looking off to the side when the shot was fired. No part of my peripheral vision had caught anything I could use to make a credible ID. But the fact that Reuben's magic fueled some sort of spell with the bullet gave me a place to start.

The condo living room flooded my senses and I was grateful I'd already been sitting down. Still, my vision swam, and I bent over sucking in air to keep from puking. A 'clink' told me someone—probably Jacquie—put a glass of water on the table beside me. I reached for it and caught a glimpse of a decidedly male hand pulling away.

My heart stopped for a moment, hoping Des had finally decided to make an appearance. Instead though when I lifted my head, I caught J.T.'s concerned gaze as he stood beside the couch in his paramedic uniform.

"You're supposed to be working a double," I said, after sucking down a large gulp of water.

"You were in that weird ass trance for hours, Ezri. I had to call him," Jacquie said from across the room.

"What? No, it was only like twenty minutes," I argued.

J.T. showed me the time on his phone. It had been early afternoon when we'd gotten here. It read 8:12 p.m. *Shit.* "I didn't realize it was that long. I'm sorry."

"Want to tell me what you were doing?" J.T. prodded. He might not be a cop, but he spent enough time around them to pick up the interrogating tone.

"It was for a case," I evaded the real question.

"Jacquie says you aren't working any active cases," he said, eyeing my partner.

She didn't look apologetic. "I really didn't mean to freak you out. It's kind of like another world when I go into someone's memories, even my own," I said.

"Ez, please, tell me what is going on. I can help," J.T. protested, sitting beside me and gripping my left hand between both of his. I felt the weight of the engagement ring more acutely than I ever had before.

"I was trying to see if there was anything I might have missed about Des' shooting."

"So, you went into your own memory without back-up." It wasn't a question.

"Believe me, I wasn't happy about it either," Jacquie muttered.

"You can both be mad at me later. I found something. I picked up the scent of someone's magic ... Reuben Wickham."

"The guy who took Carly and the others?" J.T.'s brow furrowed. "Are you sure?"

"Positive. I don't know if he was the shooter, but I know his magic was involved. It was like it was embedded inside the bullet. Which means I need to pay him a visit."

"Not tonight you don't. Besides, for all of his brushes

with the law, we can't even find his home base," Jacquie quipped.

I had other ways of finding him. "I'm going to get some air. I'll be back." I kissed J.T. on the lips and squeezed his hands.

"I promise, I'm not going to go charging into a face-off with that bastard ... Not without you," I told Jacquie as I donned a jacket, not giving either of them any time to stop me or talk me out of it.

Time to see a bartender about a douchebag.

THREE

Despite the chilly air, the line to get into Notre Dame—the one magical bar I'm aware of—was down the block. I'd left my badge at home and settled in behind a couple college kids I suspected were using fake IDs to get in. The bouncer combed the line, ostensibly checking all of those IDs. He got to me and I flashed him a smile.

"Remember me?"

"Hasn't the boss banned you yet?" He huffed.

"Nope," I answered brightly.

He looked at the long line, then back to me and hooked a thumb over his shoulder. "I don't need this tonight. Just go in and try not to blow the place up this time."

I gave him a mock bow and bypassed the line of shivering patrons. I ignored the glares from some of the girls in tight miniskirts and ankle boots. Not my problem if they chose to freeze their asses off trying to get in. I suspected the bar's owner had cast some sort of spell on the place to make it more attractive to the college crowd.

I let the warmth of the interior wash over me and took the time to cleanse my magical palette. The sandalwood charm that hung beneath the pentacle pendant around my neck was smooth against the pad of my thumb as the vestiges of my own magic vanished.

I didn't expect to find Reuben in a place like this. I settled at the end of the bar closest to the doorway and did a visual sweep of the room. When I turned back a bottle of cider sat in front of me. A slender brunette with a turtleneck stepped back from me and gestured down the bar.

"Boss says it's on the house."

I took a swig and set it down on the napkin beneath it. "You must be new here," I said.

"Just helping out for a few weeks," she answered.

The shape of her face and her coloring suggested she and Jonathan, the bar's owner, were related.

"Let me guess, uncle?" I nodded toward Jonathan.

She smirked. "That obvious?"

I leaned in and stage whispered, "I'm a cop. It's kind of my job to notice things like that."

Her cheeks flushed. "Oh, you're her, aren't you? The ... Savior?" Her voice dropped to a barely audible whisper on the last word.

"I see my reputation precedes me, again."

"You harassing my niece?" Jonathan loomed behind her in seconds.

I caught the waft of his lemon-scented magic keeping his natural form hidden. His facade of the tough guy bartender was intimidating enough. I suspected people might not come here if they knew the handsome face was attached to a literal hunchback.

"Just getting to know the new staff." I nodded toward the turtleneck. "I approve of the new work uniforms. Everyone should dress more weather appropriate."

"Missy go check on the kegs in the back," Jonathan ordered.

Missy gave me a small wave before disappearing. Jonathan rested his thick forearms on the bar. "Why are you back in my bar, Savior?"

"Can't a girl just come to enjoy a drink and the ambiance?" I replied.

"With you, no."

"How many Order members are in here tonight?"

He laughed and shook his head. "You aren't starting any more fights in my bar."

"If I thought the person I was looking for would actually show up here, I'd say I couldn't promise anything. However, since I know he's not, I can safely say I'm not going to start any fights. But I'd still like to know the answer to my question."

"I don't know. Ten, maybe fifteen."

"And how many would you say come through regularly?"

"Look, I've told you before, I don't give two shits how they practice their craft as long as they aren't slinging it around in here."

"I'm not saying you do. But I would still like the answer. Consider it, professional curiosity."

"At least triple that," he huffed spinning my cider bottle between his fingers. For a split second I thought he was going to pick it up and drink from it. "Come to think of it, business has been pretty steady, but the number of mundanes coming in has increased."

Interesting.

I wasn't sure yet, what that meant. Despite that it felt like it was important to my detective's instincts. Jonathan set the cider back down in front of me. "I heard about your friend. The cop shrink. I'm sorry."

"He was my cousin," I said, my tone going cold and steely.

"I'm even more sorry. No one should go out that way."

"Believe me, I couldn't agree more. You ever hear anyone drop the name Reuben Wickham around here?"

Jonathan's gaze narrowed. "Don't make me take back my gratuity and make you pay for that drink, Detective."

"I'll take that as a yes. Know where I might find him?'

"I do not. Just because folks associated with him hang here, doesn't mean I know everyone."

"You are a very observant man. It's why I like you," I said, hoping I could butter him up enough to get him to spill whatever he knew on Reuben's location.

"And what does that investigative nature tell you right now?" He leaned in close.

"That you want me out of your bar."

"Guess they made the right choice giving you that shiny Detective's badge after all."

"And I'd be happy to give you what you want, if you could just help a girl out."

He growled, low in his throat, but gestured to a man at the other end of the bar. "Dominic Janty. As far as I can tell, he's an acquaintance of your Mr. Wickham. Whatever you're going to do ..."

"I know, I know ... not in your bar," I finished for him.

After an awkward pause, he slammed his fist on the edge of the bar, making my bottle of cider jump. "Really, I am sorry for your loss. Family is all we've got in this world."

I downed the rest of the drink and set the empty bottle back on the bar, sliding a twenty under it. "Consider it a tip for your very nice niece."

I committed Dominic's name to memory. I couldn't tip my hand and simply go up to him just to get a look at his face. I'd have plenty of time to look him up in the database when I got to the precinct in the morning. Only it would be better if I could follow his magic.

I pushed the beginning of a buzz from the alcohol away, reaching out with my magical senses. The citrus flavor of Jonathan's' magic warred for my attention, but I shoved it aside, narrowing my search to along the bar, hoping to find the scent of Janty's magic wafting off him. Powerful men like Wickham and his ilk no doubt saw throwing around magic as no big deal. Despite that it also meant I had a better chance of tracking him.

My senses bumped up against the smell of evergreen and I couldn't stop myself from sneezing. I quickly spun on the barstool in case it was loud enough to draw attention. The scent of his magic was strong, even when I stepped out of the bar and down the street. I started back toward my car when I felt a presence behind me. I stepped into the one-way exit of a storefront and reached a hand out to grab the person tailing me.

Missy yelped when my hand connected with her jacket. "I'm sorry!"

"Jeez, what are you doing?" I snapped.

"I heard you talking to Uncle Jon about Reuben Wickham. Uh ... I know where you can find him."

My gaze narrowed. "I'm listening."

"He owns a couple real estate holdings. I've been interning all semester for the project management firm he hired to oversee some construction." She held out a bar napkin with an address written on it. "His office is on the top floor."

"Why are you helping me?" Though a bit wary, I still accepted the napkin and put it in my coat pocket.

"He creeps me out. I don't know why you're looking for him, but I'm not surprised if he's done something illegal. Just don't let him find out it was me, okay?"

I patted her arm. "I swear."

As my hand connected with her ungloved one, I could feel the bubble projected by her own magic keeping her warm, fueled by the scent of sugarcane. "Can I ask ... are you?" I made a vague gesture up and down, trying not to be offensive in assuming she was hiding a physical abnormality, too.

She giggled. "No. It was a genetic thing with Uncle Jon. He can be pretty scary, huh?"

"Yeah a little. Though he's not so bad, is he?" I pointed out.

"No, he likes to make people think he's this big tough guy, but he's got a good heart underneath it all."

I nodded and left her standing on the sidewalk by the bar. At least now I had a direction to point my anger and my power.

DECEMBER 19, 2017

FOUR

J.T. was already asleep by the time I got home just after midnight. I didn't have any missed texts or calls from Avery. Either she hadn't found anything or was still mad at me for asking and was making me wait it out. I laid the napkin from Missy on the kitchen counter and started the coffee pot, listening to the soft hum of it percolating.

"You do know how to tell time, don't you?" Grandma's tone was just as judgmental as I would have expected her to be in life.

"I'm not tired," I lied, barely fighting off a yawn.

"Right, and I'm not dead," she scoffed.

She was part of me, in some weird mystical way thanks to the pendant that held some of her power, so she knew what was going on in my head just as well as I did. "I don't want to see it again," I confessed.

"Oh, Ezzie," she wrapped her arms around me, and I sunk into her semi-corporeal embrace. "Fueling yourself on coffee forever isn't going to make it any better. You need sleep."

"I'm scared," I whispered. I hadn't said anything to J.T.

or Jacquie, but going back into my memory of losing Desmond had terrified me. Sure, I'd been hoping he would just pop up with the answers. Though really, I'd been too afraid to face the loss again.

"You are tougher than you give yourself credit for. You've been through much worse than a little bad dream."

It wasn't the memory itself that scared me now. It was what manipulating it would do to my subconscious. I dreaded being haunted by the scent of Wickham's magic.

"He can't touch you in a dream," she said, reading my mind.

I shut the coffee pot off, leaving the contents untouched before traipsing to the bedroom and stripping off my jeans and shirt. J.T. mumbled incoherently as I slid beneath the covers and snuggled into the warmth of his body. I tried to let the reassuring weight of him behind me ease me to sleep as I closed my eyes.

Cool autumn air swirled around me as I stood alone on the sidewalk. The bank loomed behind me, taller than in reality. The windows glittered with sunlight, blinding me as I turned away from them. My entire body was on high alert, sensing that this was wrong.

"Desmond?" My voice echoed around me.

"Your kin is dead," a growly voice replied, stepping around the corner of the building. That same damned hooded figure I'd dreamt about in Ireland stood before me.

"You again?" I sighed.

"We are linked, you and I. Can you not feel it? My power grows as yours wanes, Savior."

"If you're so powerful, why don't you grow a pair and show me your face?"

"I am Death. And I wear many faces," the figure answered as the scenery around us shifted. The cool air

turned biting and I shivered, even though on some level I knew this wasn't real.

"You fear what you will see here, as you should," it continued, spreading its thin arms out to the side.

I watched as a figure that looked eerily like me fell to the ground, lifeless as the figure literally danced around it. Gross. "Did you miss the part where I was literally born to kick your scrawny ass?"

"You speak with conviction, but I know your mind, Savior. You carry doubts and fears within you. You are right to fear me, Savior. For you will fail in your mission."

"Failure isn't really my thing," I quipped.

The figure laughed and the sound echoed painfully in my ears, building around me until it was all encompassing. I forced my hands to stay at my sides rather than try blocking out the laughter.

"As they say, there is a first time for everything. Your allies are weakened, and you know there is little you can do to sate that desire for revenge."

Desmond's face flashed in front of me and my stomach lurched as it spoke with his voice. "You're not going to solve this one."

My hands balled into fists and I took a swing, power erupting from my body as the figure vanished.

A pair of firm hands grabbed me by the shoulders, holding me down. "Ezri, calm down. Ezri ..."

The bedroom came into view and I sat up, hands still clenched into tight fists. My heart hammered in my throat. I could feel the slick sheen of cold sweat making the sheets stick to my body as I uncurled my fingers. I winced at the deep nail marks in the meat of my palms.

Without question, J.T. held me to him and the sweet scent of honey washed over me, sticking to my frayed nerves like the real thing. I let it seep into every pore, welcoming it home like I would my own magic.

"Sorry," I mumbled. "Didn't mean to wake you up."

"Want to tell me about it?'

"Just bad dreams," I answered, nuzzling into the slope of his shoulder.

"I meant wherever it was you went to get air for four hours."

"I was just following up on something," I answered vaguely.

J.T. pushed me back to look me in the eye—an impressive feat given the dimness of the room. "No. You don't get to do this again." His voice was sharp, tinged with anger. "You don't get to shut me out." He unwound his arm from around me. "It killed me when I lost you the first time, Ez. It broke my heart that I couldn't do anything then to make the pain stop. And you're not the only one hurting now. I lost him, too. I feel it every day. But we are going to get through this pain together. You hear me?"

I blinked at him in silence. Had I been trying to push him away? I didn't think so. Yet, as I considered the statements I'd made to him last night, I could see it starting again. That innate desire to do it all myself.

"You're right. I'm sorry." I kissed him. "I guess solo vigilante mode is sort of my default when the people I love get hurt."

He settled against the pillows, propping himself up on one elbow. "Just so you know, I'm going to keep calling you out on your bullshit. It's my husbandly duty after all."

I settled back under the covers and looked at him. "We're not married yet."

"Fiancé prerogative, then."

"Okay, fine," I conceded, brushing damp strands of hair

out of my face. "I went to Notre Dame looking for some information on Wickham," I finally admitted.

"I'm guessing you don't mean you took a little trip to Paris," he said, sounding much more awake than a normal human should in the middle of the night.

"No. It's a magically inclined bar up near Boston University. The owner and I have a ... tenuous relationship."

"Meaning?"

"Meaning, I kind of accidentally set his bar on fire once. Okay, not me, but there was fire being flung around like baseballs at me. Well he wasn't happy about it and blamed me."

"So, you decided to go there again?'

"He's a good guy underneath the gruff exterior and a lot of clientele are Order members. Since I was looking for a particular member, I assumed he'd have some information ... and I was right."

"That Wickham guy," he yawned.

"Sort of. I found a guy who works with Wickham. And I have an address of where we can find Wickham. So, I'm going to try to get some more sleep before I go busting down his door."

"You aren't going in without someone having your back."

"Wouldn't dream of it," I murmured, the soothing taste of honey on my tongue and in my nose as he lulled me back to sleep.

FIVE

Thanks to J.T.'s healing touch, the rest of my night was dreamless. I woke, feeling more alert than I had in weeks. J.T. was already out of bed and I followed the smell of sizzling bacon and sausage to the kitchen. He'd rewarmed the midnight pot of coffee and laid scrambled eggs on a plate along with the breakfast meats.

"I should apologize for stuff more often," I said as I accepted the cup of coffee and dug into the food.

"Not exactly what I was hoping to hear," he replied and joined me at the table.

"I swear, I didn't realize I was doing it again," I said, taking his left hand in my right.

"That's the frustrating thing. I know you didn't, but it still doesn't mean I believe this time is going to be any different."

"Of course, it will. I'm not a teenager anymore, J.T. I know what's going on and I can do something to actually get justice for Desmond. I've learned from my mistakes."

Have I, though?

The little voice in the back of my mind taunted me,

warning that I'd easily fall back into old patterns without thinking. I'd pushed those closest to me away to pursue a lead I knew could be dangerous all because I could. No, I'd wanted to keep them safe. *Hadn't I?*

"I hope you have," J.T. finally said, the edge back in his tone.

I wasn't sure how many times or ways I could apologize before he believed me and didn't look at me with that air of suspicion. The eggs congealed in my gut, turning the food sour in my mouth. Downing the coffee in the hopes of keeping the nausea at bay, I made a beeline for the shower. The water might wash away the grime of last night's stress, but it did little to stop the chill emanating my core. The little nugget of fear that no matter how hard I tried, I wasn't going to be able to change things this time. That I'd just end up alone again.

"I'll see you tonight," I called ten minutes later as I tugged on my coat and stuffed the napkin with Missy's scrawl on it back into my pocket. "I love you."

No reply.

I tried not to think about that fact too much as I made the drive into the city, parking beside Jacquie's car. I wanted to head straight to Wickham's' office, but not putting in an appearance at the precinct for the start of shift would raise eyebrows and attract the wrong kind of attention. So, I sat in front of my computer, staring at the screen as the napkin burned a metaphorical hole in my pocket.

"So last night, how pissed was J.T. when you got back?" Jacquie wasn't usually this interested in my love life.

"Madder this morning when I sort of didn't tell him where I'd gone."

"Not a good habit to pick back up," she noted.

Just what I needed, another person reminding me I'd been slipping. "Yeah, I know."

"You want to fill me in on what happened?"

"I paid our favorite, well only, magical bartender a visit and got some information on where we can find Wickham. I know it was his magic fueling the bullet that killed Desmond. I just need to have a conversation with him."

"He's evaded arrest and charges for decades, Ezri. He's not going to suddenly open up, because you show up magical guns blazing. Things don't work that way in the real world, Ezri."

I could make him admit to what he'd done. I didn't even need him to speak. I'd just need a few minutes in private to go probing his memory to see what I could find.

A solid lump pressed against my ribs and I gasped as the thought receded. Massaging my side, I could feel the skin beneath my shirt hardening to stone. I pushed it back down with a little of my own magic. I didn't dare exhale until it was gone again. Apparently even thinking about using magic to get the truth made Taggart's dark magic perk up. His spell that was meant to turn a practitioner's magic against them, encasing them in stone, had lain mostly dormant since I'd become its host. I didn't need it rearing its ugly head now.

"It doesn't mean I can't ask some questions," I finally replied. "Besides, I have a source who claims he's engaged in some shady business dealings. Even if the DA in the past couldn't make things stick, maybe we'll get lucky."

"We've heard that one before," Jacquie answered, but stood and pulled on her coat. "Come on. If you're going to go running headfirst into danger, might as well do it before he can see us coming."

I handed her the napkin with Missy's scrawl and she

tapped the address into her GPS, setting the fastest route into the heart of the city. It took us less than ten minutes to get there. Pulling up to the curb, I checked the napkin, grateful she'd included the floor number before I looked up at the imposing building in the Financial district. I pushed my way through the revolving door and started for the bank of elevators directly ahead.

"Excuse me, Miss, you can't just go up there," the concierge called, standing up from his desk.

I unclipped my badge from my belt and waved it in his general direction. "Actually, I can."

"May I tell them who is coming?" The concierge called just as the elevator at the far end opened and I stepped inside, Jacquie hot on my heels.

"Well, that was dramatic," she commented while pressing the button for floor eight.

"I'm in a mood," I quipped with a one-shoulder shrug.

"Promise me you aren't going to make things fly around the room," she commented as the elevator ascended past the fifth floor.

"I can't promise I won't defend myself if he comes at me with magic, but I promise I won't instigate anything."

The doors slid open to reveal luxury offices situated behind frosted glass doors. It was the only business on the floor, so I marched up and pushed the doors inward. I wasn't sure what to expect as I entered. It wasn't a brunette behind the desk who looked like a deer caught in headlights. She held the phone receiver partway to her ear and I could hear the concierge's voice squawking at her over the line.

"Where can I find Reuben Wickham?" I stood far enough back for her to see my badge.

Her free hand rose and shakily pointed to the door behind her. I caught movement out of the corner of my eye and assumed she'd switched from the line in the lobby to Wickham's personal line.

The door to a conference room on the other side of the open space opened and I caught sight of Missy sitting at a table, surrounded by business men. I could see color flush her cheeks as our gazes met before I turned back to ruining Wickham's day.

"I'm busy," I heard a familiar voice bark from inside the office with the silver placard noting Mr. Wickham. I'd only ever heard his voice inside other people's memories, when he'd stolen their magic. Despite that, I knew it was him.

I gave a single knock before entering the room. A bald man with a pointed nose stared at me, phone still pressed to his ear. I froze in my tracks as I took in his face. I'd seen him plenty of times in photos when I'd been trying to pin the kidnappings on him and in the memories that I'd seen of other Authority members when he'd stolen their family's magic. However, I'd never crossed paths with Reuben Wickham in person. I had expected a sneer and a condescending expression from him. Instead all I got was confusion and a furrowed brow. It was as though he had no idea who I was.

He hung up the phone and straightened his suit jacket and tie. "Can I help you with something, Detective ..." He trailed off, leaving me to fill the awkward pause.

"Detective Trenton," I answered.

Still nothing. No light igniting in his gaze at the mention of my name. No hint of his magic coiling around him, ready to pounce. I stood there, feeling my own confusion settle over my senses.

"So, what can I do to help our city's finest?" Reuben asked.

"I'd like to know where you were on September 21ˢᵗ?" I replied, snapping back to my senses.

He reached for the phone again. "That sounds awfully accusatory, Detective. I'm not sure I feel comfortable talking to you about my whereabouts on any given day without my lawyer present."

"You have something to hide, Reuben?" I leaned forward on his desk and reached out with my magical senses this time.

A hint of strawberry tickled my nose as I sought out the vinegar scent of his magic. I could feel the ebb and flow of the world's magic around me, weaving in and out of the space my spell occupied as it brushed against Reuben's seated form. Either he was trying very hard not to react to my magic or his magic had disappeared.

"You can get your attorney down here. That's fine. I just have one other question. Does the Order of Samael mean anything to you?"

"Should I recognize it? It sounds like some hippy cult or something." I watched his facial features as he answered, hoping for a facial tick that would betray him lying to me. Except the lack of sweat on his brow or the darting of his gaze told me the words that came out of his mouth were sincere.

Jacquie cleared her throat and nodded toward the door. I gave Wickham one last look. "When you get in touch with your attorney, give me a call. I'd still like to chat about your whereabouts, Mr. Wickham." I slid my business card across the desk toward him.

He nodded in silence as Jacquie led the way out of the office and back to the elevators. She waited until we were in the elevator before rounding on me.

"What the hell was that about?'

"He doesn't have magic," I answered.

"What do you mean? I thought he was the mastermind behind the kidnappings and the stolen magic?"

"I thought so, too. But I'm telling you, I probed him, and he doesn't have any magical signature ... at least not anymore. It's consistent with what I saw with the Authority members whose magic was stolen, except they still remembered their magical heritage and everything about our world. They still understood that magic existed and had been part of their DNA. He seems to not know the first thing about the organization he served. I didn't get a good look, but how much do you want to bet his brand is gone, too."

"What are you saying?"

"I think someone, or something, took his magic and his memory along with it. I just have no idea why."

SIX

I tried to sort out what the realization meant if I was right and Wickham's magic was truly gone. Conceptually I knew it couldn't be destroyed. It still existed somewhere in the universe. Or maybe it resided in someone else. After all, the stolen magic from three months ago had gone somewhere, too.

"Do you think someone on our side went rogue?" Jacquie offered as she pulled up to a red light two blocks from the precinct.

"Maybe. I didn't sense any other magic around him so whenever it happened, it had to have been more than a couple days ago." Which meant it probably wasn't Avery taking her revenge after watching the surveillance video.

Still she wasn't the only person that Wickham had hurt in the community. Now there were families who no longer sat on the Council, because of what he and the Order had done. They couldn't take action anymore, but they had friends with magic. As much as I didn't want to believe any of them capable of stealing his magic and his memory, I knew that pain and desperation could be a powerful motivator.

Wickham had also hurt Jacquie's family. Denise might not use her magic much, but if she somehow found him thanks to Neveah, could she have taken out her pain and anger on him? "I hate to ask this, but have you talked to Denise in the last couple days?"

The light flipped to green, but Jacquie didn't move. The car behind us blared their horn as we sat stationary in the middle of the lane. "You really think my sister-in-law, who can barely keep her shit together without magic, could hunt down a man we haven't been able to pin to anything and know enough to erase his memory and take his powers?"

"I have to rule out every possibility, and there are a lot of people who would want him punished for his actions," I replied.

Another blast of the horn spurred Jacquie to move and she pressed down on the gas pedal, propelling us forward. "She's been too focused on trying to keep Neveah moving forward now that Desmond's gone. We all know she still needs therapy, but how many magical therapists do you think there are in Boston?"

Guilt washed over me in a hot wave. I'd been so focused on my own grief and inner turmoil over Desmond's death, I hadn't stopped to consider how it had affected Neveah and the other girls with their recovery. "Shit, I'm sorry. I didn't mean to bring that up."

She waved her hand at me as she pulled into the parking lot of the precinct. "You've been grieving, too. And trying to figure out how the hell you're supposed to stop some big bad monster in what, two days' time?"

I sighed. "Yeah, that's not exactly going so great." *Do I tell her about the latest dream?* "I had another of those weird dreams again. It taunted me with Desmond's face this time."

"Are there any clues in them? Symbols or places that are the same each time?"

I scrunched my nose up, trying to remember what I'd seen in Ireland. "It's always this hooded figure whose face I can't see. And every time, it tries to kill me or promises to end me or some other dramatic bullshit."

"The setting is different, too?" She prompted.

"Yeah. Back in Ireland, it was in the place where I met Aoife."

Jacquie cut the engine and climbed out of her seat. I followed after her, not expecting to find Avery standing by my desk, headphones slung around her neck.

"You were supposed to text," I said upon seeing her.

She handed me the thumb drive. "There's nothing to report. No signs of anything that I would be equipped to handle." Her tone is too even and unemotional for my liking.

I take her by the forearm and lead her down to one of the interview rooms, slamming the door shut behind me. "You found something. I can tell."

She shook her head. "I just told you I didn't find anything."

"Avery, I know we haven't known each other that long. I also know you're pissed at me for making you look at the footage, but this is important. If you found something ... if you *did* something, I need to know."

Her brow knit together. "And what exactly would I have *done*, Ezri?"

"Gone after the most likely suspect. Maybe even made him pay for what he took from you," I answered.

She jutted one hip out to the side. "And what suspect

would that be? Because all I saw on that recording was you failing to save the man I love."

"I did everything I could," I spat back at her. She'd sat there the day after he died and told me not to blame myself. I guess she'd reached the anger stage of grieving.

Her mouth opened and closed in rapid succession as I stood there across from her before her shoulders sunk and her entire posture deflated. She sunk into one of the chairs on the far side of the table and dragged her hands through her hair. "I know you did," she whispered.

I sat opposite her. "I know this is hard for you and really I'm sorry to have made you watch that. But I am trying everything I can possibly think of to get Des the justice he deserves. I thought I had found some proof of who was involved, but it may have just led to a dead end and more questions."

She looked up, blinking back tears behind her glasses. "What do you mean?"

"I went back into my memory. I picked up on a particular magical signature. But when I went to confront that person, their magic was gone—vanished. And not just their magic, their memory of ever having magic."

"How is that possible?"

"I'm not sure. I suppose if someone is powerful enough, they could affect someone in that way. But I don't' know anyone with that much ability." Not even my own ancestors could have done that.

"The magic was completely erased? That doesn't sound right. Not with what you said about the stolen magic three months ago."

"I know, but it's what I saw. I felt the absence of magic. And he didn't react when I name dropped the Order or even my own name."

Just what I needed, another mystery to solve when the world was about to go to shit. Avery studied her hands in silence for a minute and I didn't push her. I understood the anger she'd been feeling and the sense of helplessness at being left behind. It was a feeling I battled every day for years with losing my mother. A feeling that still tried to grab hold of me now.

"Are you sure he wasn't just playing you about the Order?" She finally posed.

"I could be wrong, but he sounded sincere when I asked him. But I know for a fact I sensed his magic at the scene. He did something to the bullet."

"So, what happens now?"

"I keep digging. I know that he's got some shady business practices going on. I need to look into that and see if I can at least connect him to those."

I could tell by the way her face fell that it wasn't the answer she was hoping for. "I can try to do a little digging, too," she offered.

"There isn't any video footage that needs reviewing," I commented before I realized what she was really offering. "Please don't do anything illegal or that can be traced back to us. We want this to stick and for him to go down for his part in Des' murder."

She crossed her heart. "You have my word."

"And for the love of all that is good, don't you dare put yourself in danger. Des may be dead already, but he would kill me if anything happened to you."

She gave me a watery smile. "I can't make any promises."

Someone knocked on the door, making both Avery and me jump. The door opened and I positioned myself to spring into action if needed. I relaxed when Jacquie stuck her head in. "Sorry to interrupt, but I need to borrow my partner."

I exhaled, my shoulders visibly relaxing as I stood and ushered Avery from the interview room. I waited until she was out of earshot before I turned to Jacquie "What's going on?'

"Reuben Wickham is here, with his lawyer."

SEVEN

I fought to hold in my laugh of disbelief at the fact he'd actually turned up to talk to us. This was the last place he'd ever be caught showing up voluntarily, which made the thought of his memory being wiped all the more terrifying. I tried not to get my hopes up as we walked into the interview room down the hall. Reuben sat there looking stone-faced. His lawyer, a slender man with a hooked nose and short-cropped brown hair, sat beside him. He focused in on me the moment I sat down.

"I want to go on record saying I find it deplorable that the police have been harassing my client."

"With all due respect, Counselor, we paid your client a visit this morning and all he did was request to speak to us with you present. Which we gladly agreed to," Jacquie answered coolly before I could speak and most likely insult the man.

"But now that we're all here, how about we talk about where your client was on September 21, mid-afternoon?" I inquired, gripping my pen tight enough to drain the color from my knuckles.

"I honestly don't remember," Reuben answered.

"I think you ought to try harder," I replied.

"My client recently suffered a traumatic brain injury that has affected his memory," the lawyer said.

Convenient. I studied the man in his dark navy suit and tie. The collar and shirt sleeves were just high and long enough to cover any potential Order brand. I gathered a tiny bit of will and put it out in the world, directed at the attorney. It was just enough of a push to disrupt the placement of his shirt. I caught the barest hint of something dark on the man's left wrist. It could easily be the swirl of the triple spiral and scythe that marked the Order.

"So, was this accident which resulted in this injury recent?" I probed.

Reuben shook his head. "No. It was a ... car accident ..."

"Three months ago," the lawyer filled in. "The details are still a bit hazy for my client."

"I see. I'm assuming there's an accident report or 9-1-1 logs to verify the accident?" I gave the lawyer my best just-doing-my-job smile.

"I'm sure we can find something to satisfy you, Detective," the lawyer answered.

"What is it that you think I did?" Reuben asked unprompted.

"Reuben, keep your mouth shut." His lawyer stood up and tugged on Reuben's arm to bring him along with him.

"We're investigating a murder," I offered.

There was no recognition in Reuben's eyes as his lawyer led him away. I was about to lament the pointlessness of the exchange to Jacquie when the interview room vanished, replaced by a field covered in dirty snow.

"I don't have time for whatever mind games you're playing."

"I merely wanted to applaud you, Savior. You are relentless in your pursuit, even if you will fail in the end. We both know our destiny is a mere two days away and yet you spend your time chasing ghosts while I prepare for battle." The figure stood just out of view behind a grove of barren trees. It almost looked like it could be the Common.

"What makes you think I'm not preparing?" I replied.

The figure stepped into view and tapped its cloaked head. The sleeve slid back to reveal scarred flesh. "I see your mind, Savior. I see all of its preoccupations with the loss you suffered. It will be your downfall. Just as I will be your undoing."

"You took Reuben Wickham's magic, didn't you? And his memories. Why?"

The figure laughed and disappeared.

"I'll see what I can pull," Jacquie said as the room came rushing back around me. "What just happened?"

"That thing, the monster or whatever it is I'm supposed to stop. It keeps head hopping, paying me visits."

"What did it say"?

I wiped the sweat from my upper lip and exhaled slowly. "That I'm wasting my time trying to find Desmond's killer when I should be preparing for our fight to come."

"It's just trying to mess with your head," she said.

I nodded. "Except, it's not wrong. I don't want to face what's coming, because honestly I'm scared of what it means, Jacquie. Magic has asked so much of me and I did it all, because I figured I had no choice. But this Death's child creature is powerful. And if it in fact took Reuben's magic and his memory of magic, then it's way more powerful than I am. Solving Des' murder seems so much easier in comparison."

"You are a strong woman, Ezri. You have endured far

more than anyone in your position should have to and still you kept fighting. Do not let this thing make you second-guess yourself. Besides, you aren't alone. You've got allies and we will all be there fighting by your side."

I forced a smile. "Thanks, partner."

"Now, how about we go figure out if Reuben's telling the truth about this car accident?"

I wanted to focus on poking holes in Wickham's story, but I couldn't shake the latest visit from that creature. Also, as much as Avery was still mad at me, I worried she'd take matters into her own hands.

"Anything?" Jacquie prodded, pulling me out of my own head.

"I've got nothing," I reported to her half an hour later as I slumped back in my seat.

Before Jacquie could answer, my phone rang with an incoming call, the ring tone the one I'd assigned Avery.

"Hey, so I may have kind of broken that promise. But I think there's something you might find helpful," she said.

"I'll take whatever you've got."

"So, I might have taken a peek at Wickham's bank and credit card statements. It looks like he had dinner a few months ago at a pricey steakhouse in the city not far from the bank. One of those places with a private event space. Someone may have called the place and pretended to be his assistant. They said that it had been a big work event. Lots of people in suits."

"Okay, so he had a business meeting three months ago."

"It was the day before Desmond's murder," Avery said. Her voice hitched on the last word.

"It could be Order related."

"The woman I spoke to said that it had been a standing reservation until then. They stopped coming after that day."

Had Avery just stumbled onto the Order's meeting spot? I'd been trying to cut the head off the snake for months, but hadn't had any luck tracking them down. If she was right and they'd been holding meetings at a swanky restaurant right under my nose, well, I was pissed. It also seemed overly flashy of them to hold secretive meetings there about magic.

"Thanks for the info. I'll check it out.'

"There's one other thing." Her voice trailed off.

"Yeah?"

"I had a thought and it's probably crazy, but just hear me out. That woman you met a few months back, Adrian's cousin."

"The necromancer?" I whispered the last word.

"Yes, what if we paid her a visit? She can communicate with the dead. Maybe we could talk to him that way?"

Her browsing history about seances made sense now. I wasn't exactly Natalia's favorite person, but I was desperate for answers, too, so I'd give anything a try. "I'll call you when I'm done here and we can check it out together."

I ended the call and turned to find Jacquie staring at me. "What have we got?"

"A possible lead on where Wickham was the day before the murder." I rolled my chair around the desk to sit beside her. "Apparently, he and a lot of other very powerful people met monthly at one of those high-end steak places in the city. They were there the day before Des was shot. And they haven't been back there since."

"So, you think that whatever happened to him could have happened there?"

"Very possible. I may know how to find out, but it will have to wait until tonight."

"Why?"

"Because his associates don't go day drinking at magical bars."

"I thought you said Jonathan kicked you out last time."

"No, he just very forcefully asked me to leave his niece alone. It's not my fault she followed me and wanted to chat."

"So, he has a niece now?"

My brow furrowed. "I didn't mention that? Sorry."

Her glare softened. "I'll meet you there at eight. I have some things to take care of."

I opened my mouth to ask her what she could possibly be doing, but stopped short. There were plenty of non-suspicious things my partner could be doing. Besides, it gave me plenty of time to meet up with Avery and pay Natalia Baptiste a visit.

EIGHT

Approaching Natalia's shop made my stomach hurt. Not because the thought of dealing with someone who communicates with the dead worried me. No, it was because the last time I'd been here, she'd lied to me. She'd come to me saying she thought her cousin was dead before he'd actually died. So, I didn't trust her.

Avery stood outside the shop and she raced toward me as I approached. "I know you don't have the greatest history with her, so thank you for agreeing to try anyway."

"If she's willing to help, I'll let her." I wrapped my fingers around the sandalwood charm at my throat and inhaled deeply. Washing away the lingering bits of magic I'd done earlier in the day and to prepare myself for the blend of magics within the shop.

When I opened my eyes, the door was already swinging shut behind Avery. I followed her inside. For a moment the memory of Jacquie standing beside me, ready to question this woman about her connection to the kidnappings that led to her cousin's death washed over me.

"Can I help ... you?" Natalia's voice hitched when our gazes met.

"You might be the only one who can," I replied and stepped up to the counter. I'm sure there were other necromancers in the city, but she was the only one I had any sort of rapport with, tenuous as it may be.

"I don't know what you think I've done this time. Detective, I assure you; I've been staying away from surprise relatives."

"I'm not here in an official capacity. We need your help."

Her shoulders lowered an inch and she exhaled. "You're looking to commune with a passed loved one?"

"Yes. My husband," Avery chimed in.

"And you're here because?" She prompted, looking back to me.

"Because he was my cousin and he was murdered. I'll be damned if I let whoever did it get away."

Natalia sucked in her lower lip, studying me and then Avery. "If he was murdered, whatever I find out could be upsetting. Are you prepared for that?'

"I was there when he died. I've lived it," I answered, ice trickling into my tone.

"Oh ... I'm so sorry, Detective."

"Our family has something of a special connection to each other, even in death. Except it isn't working, and I need to know if there's anything he can tell me about the moments right before it happened."

"I can try, but sometimes when someone has died in such a brutal way, they don't want to talk. They're scared to share that with the ones they left behind."

"Desmond won't be," Avery interjected.

Natalia nodded slowly. She then gestured for us to step

around the edge of the counter and follow her back into the heart of the shop. I don't know what I was expecting, but it wasn't the comfortable set of chairs and sofa in a warmly lit room.

"Have a seat. Do either of you have something that belonged to Desmond?"

Avery handed over his wedding ring. Before I realized it, I was twisting my own engagement ring around my finger. Natalia cupped the ring in both of her palms and sat on the sofa. She settled back against the plush maroon cushions and closed her eyes.

"I'm going to need you both to be as relaxed as possible. And try not to do any magic."

Easier said than done. My own magic flared in response as soon as it sensed Natalia's power reaching out into the ether. I gripped the arms of the chair and focused on the feel of the material beneath my fingers as a way to distract myself from trying to decipher and unravel the spell she was weaving.

Without warning, she sat up and the ring fell from her hands, landing without a sound on the rug at her feet. "I'm sorry, I can't."

"He's been dead for three months. Maybe you just have to try harder," Avery said.

Natalia shook her head, her eyes glittering with unshed tears. "No, I mean, I can't find him."

"What does that mean?" My hands dug into the arms of the chair to keep me seated.

"Usually, when I reach out to the spirit realm, they come running. Even the ones who are reluctant to speak at least show up, because the object calls to them. But it's like he's not even *in* the spirit realm."

"Is that even possible? I know he's dead. I felt the life go out of him," I snapped.

She bent over and picked up the ring again. "Let me try one more thing." This time she pressed the ring between her palms before swaying back and forth. Her magic, the earthy scent of thyme, leapt out, butting up against my own defenses. The pendant around my neck grew warm and I clutched at it, strawberries blossoming all around to protect it.

Natalia inhaled sharply and her eyes flew open. "This may not make sense to you, but I felt him, or at least his magic, within you."

"Is that a thing?" Avery prompted.

"No." Not exactly, anyway. Only Desmond had bound his magic to an object right before his death and poured the rest of his power into the pendant as he was dying. So, maybe because his magic was still bound here, he wasn't in the spirit realm yet.

"All I can do is tell you what I sense and he's not in a place where I could reach him. I'm sorry I couldn't help you. Truly I am. I know the pain of losing someone you love unexpectedly."

"Have you ever had that happen before? Someone dead who isn't in the spirit realm?" Avery prodded.

Natalia shook her head. "No. Never. I've had reluctant souls, sure. But they've always been there, somewhere. Your husband just isn't."

I tried not to let the anger bubbling beneath the surface erupt. Part of me wanted to blame her for not trying hard enough, but I could also tell that she was telling the truth. Something deep inside me, or maybe it was the pendant, confirmed her statements. I was angrier with Desmond for making all of this so damn complicated. Didn't he want to be at peace?

"Thanks for trying anyway," I said and stood up.

"Detective, I know you blame me for what happened with Adrian. And I know I deserve some of that blame. I should have realized that something was off after not hearing from him for so long. But I have to believe if he were still alive, he would regret what he did."

"Guess he's lucky he's dead then," I muttered.

NINE

I waited for Avery to join me. When she appeared her face was resigned, and she kept her gaze cast down. "I'm sorry I dragged you here for basically nothing," she said once we were outside.

"It was worth a shot," I answered just as my phone buzzed with an incoming text from J.T. I swiped to open the message to find a bunch of emojis which I interpreted to mean he wanted to go out for dinner.

"I'll let you know if anything else comes from looking into the Order," I said and stepped away to give him a call.

"So, I'm guessing that's a no to dinner?" J.T. said when he picked up.

"I've got plans with Jacquie tonight at eight, but if it's beforehand I'm totally in," I answered.

"I'm off shift at four. I can run home and change. Then meet you wherever you want."

I had a place in mind. "Hope you've got some extra cash laying around, because the place I'm thinking of is pretty high-end."

"After everything we've been through, we deserve it. Text me the address and I'll meet you there."

"It's a date."

Visiting Natalia had been a bust, but maybe dinner with my fiancé was exactly what I needed. I had a couple hours to kill before then, so I headed home to get ready. Avery still loitered on the sidewalk, like she was waiting for me to dismiss her.

"We're going to figure this out," I said, hoping my words were enough to keep her from running off and trying anything crazy.

"I was just so sure she'd be the answer," Avery sighed and pushed her glasses up her nose. Finally giving me a small wave, she trudged up the street away from the shop.

The drive home was eerily silent. I couldn't help glancing at the pendant's reflection in the rearview mirror as I pulled into the parking spot. *Had I screwed things up for Des by trying to keep his magic safe?*

Standing in front of the bedroom mirror an hour and a half later trying to get my eyeliner just right reminded me of how much time I don't take for myself. I hadn't gotten dressed up like this, let alone gone out on a date in months. Not since before Desmond's death. Part of me feared that any celebration of the life J.T. and I were going to start together dishonored his memory and that I shouldn't be celebrating.

"You look amazing," J.T. said from the doorway.

I fumbled the eyeliner pencil and turned to look at him, my cheeks burning in embarrassment. "I feel kind of silly all dressed up."

He closed the distance between us, still in his paramedic uniform and pulled me in for a kiss. "We could always just say to hell with a fancy dinner and stay in." His serious bedroom eyes told me in no uncertain terms just what his idea of a night in entailed.

"We should go out and enjoy ourselves though," I replied, leaning back against his embrace to study his face.

"So, what are these plans you've got with Jacquie tonight?" He began unbuttoning his shirt and I couldn't help ogling him. The shirt hit the floor, revealing the flimsy undershirt covering his chest and upper arms.

"Uh, a work thing," I answered as he tugged the undershirt off.

"Got it," he said and went hunting through the closet for a dress shirt. I wanted to protest, to say that he was right, and we should never leave the apartment, but I needed to see what I could find out about the Order's meeting place.

"Not everything has to be about work you know," Grandma's voice said from off to my left.

"You have terrible timing," I ground out through pursed lips.

"What'd you say?" J.T. asked, turning around as he buttoned the sleeves of his shirt.

"Nothing. I need to go to the bathroom, then I'll be ready to go," I said and darted out for the room.

Grandma was already present when I slammed the door shut. "Seriously, I am glad you aren't alive, because holy crap you are such a buzzkill."

Her aviators slid down the bridge of her nose. "Girl, you're the one forcing yourself to drag that very sweet man outside in the cold to dig for answers that you yourself don't really believe will be there."

"I am not," I answered, but I knew the words were total bullshit the moment they left my mouth.

"I'm trying to get justice for Desmond, and I keep

hitting walls. But don't I owe it to him to keep trying? To keep searching?"

"Course you do, Ezzie. But that doesn't mean you can give up your own life, your own happiness in the process. Now, either keep that man home all night or just enjoy a fancy dinner together. Leave the work and the justice seeking at the door for a few hours."

I wanted to argue, but I knew I'd been beaten. She was right. I'd been burying myself in Desmond's case just like I had my mother's. I could say I was keeping J.T. in my life this time, but I was only using our relationship to get what I wanted. He deserved better than that.

"You okay in there?" J.T. called through the closed door.

"Fine," I answered and checked my hair before opening the door. "We don't have to go if you don't want to," I blurted, taking in the fact not only was he in a dress shirt, but he'd put on a jacket and tie.

"You wanted to go out, so we go out."

I bit my lower lip. "I kind of suggested this place, because it might be a meeting place for higher-level Order members ... and it's related to me digging into Desmond's case."

"Ezri, I have known since you suggested it. You don't think I knew there was a reason you wanted to go to one of the highest price steakhouses in the city out of nowhere?"

"You did?"

"Am I happy you couldn't just tell me the truth? No. But, honestly, I'm used to it. It's part of who you are, for better or worse. And I'm pretty sure that's part of the vows we are going to make to each other."

I shook my head and leaned in to kiss him. "I really don't deserve you. But, I promise, no sleuthing while we are there. Just a nice dinner."

"I'm going to hold you to that. Now come on, our ride is waiting."

"What ride?"

He grinned. "You'll see."

I wasn't expecting the freaking limo sitting outside in our parking lot. If he hadn't already proposed to me three months ago, I would have suspected he was going to pop the question tonight. I let him help me in and accepted the tiny glass of champagne sitting on the limo bar.

"To us," he toasted and clinked glasses.

"To us."

The bubbles fizzed in my nose and it took everything I had not to sneeze into the glass. Some types of alcohol just don't agree with me. J.T. sat beside me and scooped my left hand into his right, running his finger over the band on my ring finger.

"I know things haven't been normal since Desmond died, but I have to believe he'd want us to be happy, right?"

"Of course, he would," I answered leaning my head against his shoulder.

"I know you aren't one to rush into decisions and you asked to put things for our wedding on hold, but we still don't know exactly what you're facing."

I smiled and felt tears prick the backs of my eyes. "I've been thinking the same thing actually," I admitted.

"You have?" He shifted to gaze down at me.

"Yeah. I know what I said and all, but the truth is I think I was just trying to deny whatever was coming. And I don't really want to have to plan a wedding. It's too much drama figuring out who to invite, and who sits where and all that stuff. I just want it to be us, maybe some witnesses down at City Hall." My cheeks flushed as the words fell out of my mouth. I hadn't wanted to acknowledge those feelings, especially not to him. I didn't want to crush his expectations.

"That's all I want, too. Our families and close friends. Whatever is coming for you, I don't want you to face it alone. I want to be there with you, as your husband."

I smiled up at him and a giddy laugh escaped. "So uh, how about we take some time off tomorrow and get married?"

"Sounds perfect."

The limo stopped and the driver climbed out of the vehicle, rounding the back to open our door. He offered me a gloved hand and I took it, giving him a little curtsy as I stepped onto the curb. I had never felt so important before and I was the Savior of the whole magical community. J.T. stepped up beside me and wrapped an arm around my shoulders before ushering us inside and out of the cold.

As the revolving door spun behind us, I came to a very important realization. Wanting to eat here, no matter the reason, was all well and good, but it probably took reservations months in advance.

"Two, under the name Somers," J.T. said casually to the hostess.

She glanced down at her chart and gave a nod. "May we take your coats?"

"Thank you," he replied and slid mine off my shoulders. He started to offer my purse to the coat check when I snatched it back. I was meeting Jacquie later on police business and this dress didn't exactly have lots of places to hide a gun. I didn't normally keep it in my purse, but I figured J.T. would be upset about the thigh holster.

"Right this way," she said and waved us past the podium.

"How the hell did you get a reservation here on like two

hours' notice?" I whispered as we followed the woman past large round tables for six or eight people and into the back at a cozy table for two.

He waited until the hostess had seated us before answering. "I got lucky. My partner Lily pulled an extra shift a couple months ago, saved the life of one of the owners of this place. I got her to pull in a favor to get us a reservation short notice."

"I knew there was a reason I loved you," I sighed.

He kept smiling at me across the candle-lit centerpiece, the sort of dopey school-boy grin that I couldn't help but mirror back to him. I'd been so focused on all the negative things in my life, I had forgotten to relish the good.

"I know you promised to not focus on work tonight while we're here, but have you found anything else out that could help solve the case?"

I shook my head. "Only dead ends. Reuben Wickham has completely lost his magic. And his memory of ever having it. I thought maybe Avery might have gone a little rogue, but it happened way before she knew anything about him being involved. And we went to see this necromancer, Adrian's cousin. But she couldn't sense Desmond in the spirit realm."

"What does that mean?"

"She wasn't sure, other than it had never happened before. I don't know, maybe since he bound his family magic to an object and because he put the rest of his power into the pendant he's bound here somehow? I just wish he'd show his face and talk to me."

"For a therapist, he wasn't the best at communicating with other people sometimes," J.T. mused.

"I may have had issues, but he had his own drama, too."

The conversation halted as a waiter in a navy vest and

tie appeared to take our drink orders and deliver menus. It was so perfectly normal, I tried to cling to it and savor everything.

"So, what sounds good? I was thinking steak. It is a steakhouse after all," J.T. rambled adorably across the table.

"I was going to go all seafood." I glanced at the prices and paled. "Or not."

"Get whatever you want. Don't worry about the price," J.T. said and squeezed my hand.

"Are you sure?"

"Absolutely."

Lobster tail and crab legs with a side of sautéed shrimp it is. Our waiter reappeared with our drinks and dutifully took our order before disappearing from view again. I took the time to survey our surroundings. It was a well-appointed dining area with soft neutral tone carpeting and warm wood paneled walls. The lighting was set at just the right level to be inviting, but not too bright or too dim to impact reading. Even the music was kept at a respectable level and played some light classical tune I didn't recognize.

"I'll be right back, I need to find the bathroom," I announced.

Our waiter materialized at my side, making my heart skip a beat. I was about to accuse him of eavesdropping when I realized he was already bringing our meals.

"Is everything all right, Miss?"

"Yes. Just need to make a trip to the ladies' room," I answered, trying to get my heart to calm down.

"Very good. Take the spiral staircase up to the second floor. It is the last door all the way on the right when you reach the landing.'

"Great, thanks." I turned to J.T. "There better still be food on my plate when I get back."

He feigned a wounded look. "I would never."

I shook my head at his expression and marched up the stairs to follow the waiter's directions. I paused at a door marked 'Private.' I could hear voices from within. They were low, but still audible. I was about to ignore them when the word 'magic' caught my ear. I knew I shouldn't listen in. It could be a discussion about anything. They might not even be talking about real magic. Yet, my curiosity got the better of me.

"Just for a minute," I murmured to myself.

A high-pitched female voice was speaking. "Are we really going to let this go on?"

"Like we have a choice? You want to go up against ... that *thing*?"

"I happen to like remembering all of this." As the woman spoke the last word something clattered beyond the closed doorway and I could swear I caught a whiff of aloe.

Definitely real magic.

The reference to a thing and memory signaled Reuben's odd condition in my mind. Maybe he hadn't been the only one affected back before Desmond's death? If that was the case, perhaps that death creature was slowly siphoning magic from the rest of the Order? But why?

"I have to get going. I'm late for another meeting," the man said, and I could hear the abrupt scrape of chair legs against the floor.

I turned, not wanting to be caught and remembering I actually needed to use the bathroom when I spotted Theodora Harrow standing at the end of the hallway. I hurried toward her and found the door to the women's room. I darted inside to find the rest of the stalls empty.

"You have some insight you just couldn't wait to share?" I whispered.

"You made a promise to your betrothed that you would leave the mystery unsolved for the evening," she quipped. For the first time since she'd begun popping up in June, she gave me a disapproving look.

"I didn't break that promise. I just lingered before coming in here." I gestured to the nearest stall. "Speaking of, do you mind? I do actually have to go."

She turned her back and I slid into the stall. "So, do you have any idea how this creature could be removing every-one's entire memories of magic?" I sort of understood the mechanics behind removing their memories of the attack, but to take their entire recollection of magic itself seemed unnecessarily cruel. Especially if that memory loss spread down through the victim's entire family tree.

"I am afraid I have never witnessed such magic being done. After the trials, we had to keep our gifts hidden away. Even the Order was subtle in their methods at the start." She stopped speaking. Only with the way her words fell off, I could tell she wanted to say something else.

"Whatever it is, I'm a big girl and I can take it," I said and stepped out of the stall over to the tiny sink.

"I think you may be distracting yourself with trying to right a wrong instead of preparing for the battle that looms."

"You sound like that thing who keeps showing up in my head."

"I can feel the fear it instills within you. I do not have such an aim. I want you to be ready to face whatever comes."

"But how can I face it if I don't know what really happened to Desmond?" I swallowed the lump in my throat as a thought flashed through my brain. "What if this is the last chance I've got?"

"You believe you will be asked to pay the price of a

life?" Theodora's voice diminished so much in pitch I almost thought I'd imagined it.

"Something about the words the last of Harrow's blood flowing forevermore doesn't exactly instill me with hope." Maybe I'd avoided trying to figure out the prophecy this long, because I didn't want that to be the outcome. I was only twenty-five years old, far too young to die.

"My sister was not much older than you when they hung her," Theodora breathed.

"It's not a trend I'm eager to continue."

"May I pose a different question?"

I gestured for her to continue and she clasped her hands in front of her.

"If the Order has been dismantled in this way, is that perhaps a good thing?"

"I have no love lost for them. They're a bunch of greedy assholes who enjoy hurting people for fun. And I can't say I'm broken up about some of the heavy hitters being taken out of play, but magic is part of a person's makeup, just like their eye color or hair color. It's not supposed to be stripped away. There may be less evil in the world, but if this death creature is actually stealing their power, it's increasing its own and that is far more dangerous."

"You may be correct," she sighed.

"I need to get back to J.T. before he decides I've drowned in the toilet and steals my food."

That at least brought a smile to Theodora's lips before she disappeared. The pendant around my neck warmed slightly against my skin and I took it to mean she was having a good laugh at me with the rest of the family.

When I descended the stairs by our table, I saw J.T. poking at his steak.

"Sorry about that," I apologized as I settled across from him.

He looked up from his food. "Are you okay?"

I leaned closer to the candle flickering between us and whispered, "Impromptu family reunion." I tapped the pendant for emphasis.

"Who showed up this time?"

"Theodora. She thinks I'm distracting myself with chasing down Des' killer to avoid what's coming. I can't say she's entirely wrong. But, if this prophecy is as big as it feels, I may not have another chance to do right by him."

He set his fork and knife down and reached across the table to hold both of my hands. "I won't lie, I've been working more to try and distract myself from the fact that the Solstice is only two days away. I don't want to lose you."

Tears welled up behind my eyes again, but I refuse to let them fall. I can't promise him everything will be fine or that I'll come home to him when all of this is over. "I don't want to lose you either."

I could give him a little bit of happiness before everything went to shit. So, I gave his hand a squeeze before diving into the pile of seafood on my plate and focusing on our date.

TEN

With my belly full of expensive food and wine, I made my way to Notre Dame to meet Jacquie. I didn't know if Dominic Janty would be present, but if he was, I wanted to have a chat with him to see what he knew about Reuben's whereabouts the day of Desmond's death. I spotted Jacquie standing near the front entrance, chatting with the burly bouncer.

"You're like a damn bad penny," he barked at me when I was within earshot.

"I'm just here for a girls' night," I add and looped my arm through Jacquie's. Thankfully she rolled with it.

"I'll call you," Jacquie said as she led me into the bar.

"Were you seriously flirting with that guy?" I said just loud enough for her to hear me over the music.

"If I wanted to get in here tonight, you bet I was."

I relaxed a little at her statement. "So, uh, before we go hunting for bad guys, are you busy tomorrow afternoon? It's for a personal thing." I propped myself up against the edge of the bar scanning the crowd.

"I don't know, depends on if the bad guys decide to take a day off. Why?"

I fiddled with the engagement ring on my finger. "J.T. and I are going to City Hall to get married ... and I was hoping you'd be there."

She spun around to stand on my other side, and I could see the sparkle in her eye. "I thought you were waiting for all of this magic shit to blow over."

"We both kind of figured, what's the point in waiting. Neither of us wants a big thing so this just makes sense."

She beamed at me. "Of course, I'll be there." She turned to look around the bar when I heard the sound of a glass clinking against the bar behind me. I pivoted, ready to feed Jonathan another line about it being a free country so I could frequent his bar if I wanted. Instead though I found Missy standing opposite me.

"Oh, hey," I greeted.

"Did that thing I mentioned work out?"

"Still a work in progress," I said cagily.

"Oh ..." She cast her gaze down at the bar. "Sorry I couldn't help more."

"Hey, you helped quite a lot. In fact, I'm here hoping to meet with a friend of his, Dominic Janty. Do you know him?"

Missy nodded toward a high-top table across the dance floor where a blonde in a low back dress sat beside a man with a drink in his hand.

"I finished checking accident reports and there's no evidence Reuben was in one," Jacquie said in my ear just as I got within an arm's length of Janty's table. I could still see the Order brand on the side of his neck. Good, he still had his memory, then.

"I'm serious, you wouldn't believe me if I told you," he

told the woman on his arm, his voice carrying over the music.

My stomach dropped. He'd been at the restaurant earlier. The woman laughed and turned just enough for me to catch her face in profile.

Agent Cartwright?

She turned just enough to see me and the fake smile she had plastered on her face vanished instantly. She mouthed, "What are you doing here?"

I just shook my head, having no response. I didn't want to announce myself as police if other members of the Order were around. Not without any magical back-up. Besides I couldn't count on Jonathan to step in and lend a hand like last time. From Molly's other side, Jacquie took an aggressive step forward. Somehow, spilling a drink I hadn't even noticed she'd picked up all down the side of Molly's dress.

"I am so sorry," Jacquie professed, setting the glass on the table. "I just ruined your dress. Here, let me help. Or can I buy you another drink?"

I had to hand it to my partner she was damn good at undercover work. Molly, to her credit, didn't lose a beat. "I don't want your apology. How about you pay for my dry cleaning?"

She stomped off in the direction of the neon sign denoting the restrooms with Jacquie hot on her heels, still apologizing profusely. I kept my head down and stepped into the bathroom just in time to see them facing off. Molly pressed a wad of paper towels to her dress.

"What are you two doing here?" She demanded.

"Us? It's a magical bar. I've got magic," I answered. "What are you doing here talking to our mark?"

"Dominic Janty is under federal investigation for money laundering and tax fraud," she answered.

I couldn't say I was surprised by that revelation and it explained why she was there chatting him up. Except it did complicate matters, especially since I needed him to tell me what had happened to Reuben Wickham.

"He's involved in the Order," I said, my voice modulating up in pitch. "That spiral and scythe brand on his neck proves it."

"The same guys you said were behind the kidnappings? Just like the guy we could never pin to those kidnappings?"

"Yes. And the ones who were stealing magic. Except it seems like whatever monster they've created is getting greedy. At least one of their top rank players, who not only no longer has his magic, but has no memory whatsoever about the magical world. It was just stripped out of his head." A thought occurred to me. Jonathan had said more mundane people had been frequenting the bar lately. Had the creature been siphoning magic and memories from the lower ranks, too?

"Why?"

"I don't know. But I bet you Janty can fill in some of the blanks. But he'll know my face and he'll know I'm the Savior. He won't talk to me." At least I assumed he would know me. Taggart had and I very well doubted that he wouldn't have passed on the information to his buddies in the time since he'd abandoned the Authority's ranks.

"And I doubt he'll be eager to open up to the woman who just ruined his date's dress," Jacquie added.

Molly looked at each of us in turn before she sighed and pulled out her phone from the tiny purse on her wrist. "Get ready to listen in ladies."

"You don't have to do that," I said, silently doing a happy dance that she was ready to jump in and help us out.

"We're both after the same bad guy. If I can help you

get answers before we bring him in, I'm game. Besides, now I'm curious." She dialed my number and then stowed it in her purse. "Make sure you're on mute."

I pulled out my phone, answered the call and showed her that I'd hit the mute button. I eked out a little will to amplify the sound so that we wouldn't have to worry about all the background noise. Doing it here would ensure Janty wouldn't catch on.

At the door to the bathroom, she turned and addressed Jacquie. "I think you missed your calling. You'd make one hell of an undercover agent." She left us standing in the bathroom in stunned silence.

"We should wait a few minutes before we go back out there. We don't want Janty to be too suspicious," Jacquie said.

"Right. You know, she's not wrong, you would make a badass undercover officer. How come you never went that route?"

"As a detective I don't need to pretend to be someone else to do my job. I earned this badge by upholding the ideals of this department, by being fair, and protecting and serving this community. I did that by being someone people could trust. Undercover work, it's not for me."

"Agent Cartwright seems to disagree. But you'd never jump ship, right?"

Jacquie clapped me on the shoulder. "You're stuck with me, partner. For better or worse."

I snickered at her choice of words. My phone picked up the ambient noise of the bar beyond the bathroom and I could hear Molly return to Janty's table. "You all right?" His voice came over the line. My spell was working.

"The dress is probably ruined, but our night doesn't have to be. Before we were so rudely interrupted, you were telling me about that guy you used to work with. I think you said he had a massive personality change out of nowhere?"

"You don't want to hear about that stuff," he said brushing her off.

"I'm a sucker for the dramatic and this sounds like it should be extra crazy. Come on, what's the harm? It's not like he's going to find out, right?"

Jacquie and I left the bathroom and settled at the far end of the bar, the phone set between us on the counter. I pulled out a pair of Bluetooth headphones and passed one to Jacquie, syncing them and securing one in my ear. We didn't need Order members or anyone else around us hearing the conversation. I caught sight of Jonathan at the opposite end, his handsome features were hard to miss even with the magic keeping the rest of his physique hidden.

"I thought we had an understanding," he said as he approached.

"I'm here on police business and I'd really appreciate if you could back off so you don't blow our cover," I said, irritated that he was disrupting my ability to pay attention to every word coming out of Janty's mouth.

"That pretty blonde over there, she showed up the last time you damaged my establishment. This some sort of sting?"

Jacquie fixed him with a pointed look. "You are a civilian. You don't get to know the details of police operations. Now, do everyone a favor and go wait on your patrons."

"Fucking cops," he muttered, but returned to his post at the opposite end of the room.

"I wasn't there mind you, but this business associate of mine was always pretty full of himself. Like he couldn't ever lose. You know the type," Janty continued.

"Oh, I do," Molly agreed, egging him on.

"Well, a few months back he stops coming around and when he returned it's like he's a whole different person. I mean I suppose some traits are hard to get rid of. He's still kind of an asshole and thinks his shit doesn't stink. But it's like he forgot everything he'd ever done before."

"You think he's faking it?"

"Hell no," Janty responded. "It's too good a job for him to be faking it. He says he was in a car accident that totaled his car, but I did a little digging, due diligence and all, and there's nothing about it anywhere."

"So, what, are you saying he lost his memory by ... magic?" She added a hint of disbelieving laughter into her voice on the last word.

Damn, she's good.

"There's a reason I said you wouldn't believe me."

"You're serious. Magic made him lose his memory? I'd love to meet the magician who can do that. I've got some years in college I'd love to forget."

"It's not what you think." His voice dipped in volume and I strained to hear it over the phone line and the ambient white noise of the bar.

"I'm a big girl, you know. I can handle it," Molly goaded.

"Ah, what the hell!" I watched him down the rest of his drink and set the empty glass on the table. "Magic's real. But if you aren't careful, it can disappear just like *that*." He snapped his fingers for emphasis.

"What, someone just says a magic word and poof it's gone? What's the point of having magic if it can just be taken away so easily?" Molly pressed.

"It didn't used to be that way. Times are changing. There's a shift of power and it's not in the favor of the law-abiding citizens of this city."

"So, you're not one of those law-abiding citizens, then?"

"Sure, I am," he quipped. "But there are people who think just because they won the fight centuries ago, that they get to dictate how we live. History being written by the winners and all. We've been punished long enough for just living."

All he'd done so far is confirm that the death creature took Wickham's memory and his magic. I needed to know more. I needed to know why and what he knew about Wickham's involvement in Desmond's murder. Only I couldn't just go up to him and ask. Not without risking blowing Molly's cover for her own case.

"You have that look that says you want to spring into action," Jacquie said just loud enough for me to hear.

"She's not asking the right questions," I grumbled.

"She's doing the best she can without risking everything," she reminded me.

"So, what's the one thing you'd love to forget about with all this magic stuff?" Molly prodded, her voice coming in over the phone line.

"That even the side that thinks it should be used however you want is subject to bureaucratic bullshit."

"Uh oh, sounds like someone doesn't like their boss?" She teased.

"Let's just say I'm not a fan of hostile takeovers. I prefer my merger and acquisitions to be mutually beneficial.'

That's an interesting perspective I hadn't considered. I'd assumed that this death creature had been the brainchild of the whole Order, or at the very least most of their leadership. Except, then most of their plans hadn't gone the way they'd anticipated. They'd failed to raise the creature into a proper body back in March. I might not have been able to prevent the kidnappings six months ago, but at least I'd found out about the prophecy they'd been after. I'd even ensured that they didn't strip all of the Council of their magic. And yet, they were still coming. This Death's child was still haunting my dreams and invading my mind. Had it been Wickham's plan and it had just gotten away from him?

"You think this hostile takeover is the reason your buddy doesn't remember how to tie his own shoes?"

"It's a lot more complicated than that, but yeah, I'd say so. He thought he knew what he was getting into, then it came out of nowhere and ripped it all away," Janty answered.

The conversation stopped and I glanced over my shoulder to see Molly studying Janty in the strobing lights from the dance area. "You scared you'll be next?"

He laughed, but it came over the line as a hacking sound. "It's only a matter of time."

"He knows more than he's saying," I said and was off the bar stool before I realized I'd made the decision to move.

Jacquie snaked her hand out to catch me and hold me back. My sudden movement was enough to draw Molly's attention. "Get him to admit Wickham killed Desmond," I stage whispered at her.

"I don't blame you for being scared. I mean, I guess I can see how it could be scary losing part of yourself. Did you ever try to talk to your buddy about what had happened, maybe try to jog his memory?"

"What's the point? He doesn't know anything. Not about magic or our boss. None of it."

"I guess I see your point. It's not like he murdered anyone," Molly offered.

"No, he's a bastard, but he's not that evil," Janty commented.

My heart plummeted into my stomach and I sunk back

onto the stool. It wasn't the answer I'd wanted, but it was an answer. It didn't explain how his magic got on the bullet, but then again ... maybe it had? I'd been assuming this death creature didn't have a physical form, but what if it had found a body? It could wield Wickham's magic and use it as if it belonged to the creature. At least, it sounded reasonable in my head. Despite that there was one person who might be able to fill in some of the blanks.

"I have to make a trip to see Taggart," I told Jacquie as I leaned my head on the bar.

"You can't trust him."

"I know, but he's connected to all of this. If he was involved in trying to bring this creature back six months ago, then maybe he knows more about it. Believe me, he's not the person I want to be spending time with on the day I'm getting married. Yet, if he can help me put this to bed, I have to try. Besides, if I'm facing off with whatever this thing is in two days, I'm going to exhaust every avenue I can to get Des justice."

"You want backup?"

"I appreciate the offer, but this is between him and me."

I ended the call with Molly and slid a twenty on the bar as a peace offering to Jonathan. As I left the bar, I tried to remind myself that tomorrow was going to be a better day. After all, it was my wedding day.

DECEMBER 20, 2017

ELEVEN

Morning dawned and I blinked at the light filtering through the windows in the bedroom. J.T. was already gone, pulling an early morning shift to ensure we'd be able to get to the courthouse with enough time to actually get married. I lay there in the stillness of the condo and let the realization that I was getting married today settle over me. Reaching for my phone, I dialed my dad's number, not caring that it was too early.

"Ez? Is everything okay?" Dad sounded more awake than I expected.

"Yeah, everything's fine. Do you have plans this afternoon?"

"Not really, no. What's going on?"

"J.T. and I decided we're going to City Hall to get married. I want you to be there."

I could hear the smile in his voice. "I knew it! I'm so happy for you, sweetheart. Of course, I'll be there. Just let me know what time."

"We're thinking two o'clock. I know you probably were

hoping to walk me down the aisle and give me away, but this just feels right."

"I had my chance to get married how I wanted. This is your marriage, Ezri. You get to decide how it happens."

"I know I've said it a lot lately, but I'm sorry I was so terrible to you for so long."

"You've apologized enough. I should have been able to talk to you about all of it, but I got lost in my own grief and I didn't want to push you away any more than I already had. But I'm so glad we've had this time together. I know your mother would be proud of you."

"I'll see you this afternoon, Dad. Love you." I set about making myself presentable for my trip to the prison to see Taggart. After that side trip, I could spend a little more time doing my hair and make-up in preparation for the ceremony.

"I'm glad you're doing this," Grandma said from behind me.

"Happy you approve," I replied and continued applying eyeliner.

"I was worried there for a minute that it was going to be all doom and gloom til the very end. But you're doing something for yourself and you're making that young man immeasurably happy."

"Have you ... I don't know ... seen Des in there?" I gestured to the pendant. "Is he ever going to talk to me?"

"Manifestation like this takes time." She pointed to the pendant. "And while I don't know for sure how that thing works, I have to believe it gives you who you need when you need them. Even if you can't see him, you know he's here with you."

"I feel like I'm failing him by not getting the answers he deserves. To know who pulled the trigger."

"Have you stopped to consider that he isn't the one in need of those answers? That you're really the driving force behind this crusade?'

"He'd want to know the truth."

"And if you find it, what are you going to do with it? That awful Wickham man doesn't even remember magic exists or that he ever had it to begin with. He certainly doesn't know he was an accessory to kidnappings and murders."

"Then I will punish whoever still remembers," I answered sharply, slamming the eyeliner pencil down on the dresser. For a split second I could swear I smelled the nauseating scent of burning sugar. Like someone had tried to flambé strawberry and failed miserably.

"And you're sure talking with that bad FBI agent is the right move?"

"He's been involved with this since the beginning. If anyone knows what the plan was, it's Taggart. You're not going to talk me out of it. Besides, he's an asshole, but he's not stupid. He's not going to try anything while I'm there. I'm pretty sure he doesn't want to find out what solitary confinement does to a man's psyche."

"Don't lose sight of what today is supposed to be about," she said as I headed for the door, sliding my badge around my neck, pulling on my jacket and belting on my sidearm.

The city was surprisingly empty at this hour on my trip to the prison. I couldn't' shake Grandma's suggestion that Des didn't' care who'd killed him. Of course, he cared. It wasn't just me trying to tie up loose ends. *Right?* I'd been honest with Theodora last night that I didn't want to think about the prophecy, because of the possibility it meant I wouldn't be walking away from this confrontation. Maybe I did need the answers so I could face that possibility knowing I wasn't leaving anything left undone.

As I sat in my car, waiting for visiting hours to start at the prison, I could feel the weight of the world's magic shifting around me. Darkness pressed against me more than I'd felt in a long time and I shivered despite the heat blasting me in the face. Maybe it was more than just the chill in the air that was getting to me.

"You can feel it now, the power which will see you beaten," an exhaustingly familiar voice said from the backseat.

I adjusted the rear-view mirror to find the faceless shadowy figure lounging in the back seat like I was its damn chauffeur. I could see its fingers were hooked and scarred, permanently in claws. "So, you can pop up when I'm awake now, too?"

"I am everywhere. I am Death and my strength only grows. I have come to make you a simple offer. Bow down and join me, willingly grant me your power ... I will spare you and those you love."

I couldn't resist rolling my eyes. "Right, because I'm just going to believe the faceless thing that's trying to end the world as I know it. I'll pass."

The feeling of fingers running along the nape of my neck turned my stomach, threatening to grant my breakfast burrito an encore. I spun, reaching for the figure behind me, but it was already gone. The scent of ash and decay was the only thing left in its wake.

It had really been here this time. Not just a figment in my head. Maybe it was right, and it was growing in power as the Winter Solstice neared and dark magic gained its foothold in the world.

"No, it's just trying to keep you off balance, because you're getting closer to unraveling its twisted plans," I chided, shaking my head as my phone alarm blared that I could go in to see Taggart now.

The bleary-eyed officer on duty at check-in looked at me like he'd never seen another human being at this hour before. I showed him my badge. "I'm here to see Jamison Taggart."

"You have an appointment?" He barely stifled a yawn.

"Nope, but that doesn't mean I can't still request to speak with him."

He turned his attention to the computer screen just out of my view and tapped away. "You're in luck. He just got released from the Infirmary. Give me a few minutes and I'll get you checked in."

I leaned against the opposite wall while I waited, wondering what had landed him in the infirmary. I knew former law enforcement tended to be easy targets in prison. Despite that he had magic and he'd been very clear about not caring who saw him use it. Still, I thought he'd been keeping a low profile.

Some ten minutes later, I'd stowed my badge, gun, and phone in a locked container before being led through to a private interview room. I couldn't be sure, but it looked just like the one we'd been in during our last conversation six months ago. When I'd come to him asking for information on three missing children. He'd disavowed any knowledge and I'd taken him at his word then. I didn't have the luxury of believing he didn't know anything about the current situation. I settled in the rigid metal chair on one side of the table and waited.

The door opened and Taggart shuffled in, his gait hindered by shackles on his ankles and the brace on his left leg keeping it immobilized. His wrists were bound in front of him. Though it was his face that made me inhale audibly. Someone had used it as a punching bag. He sported dark bruises under both eyes conveying the broken nose even before I noted the unnatural angle. He may have tried to murder me and had used an innocent man to commit crimes for him, but I still scooted back. I wanted to give him space to stretch out his leg as much as the shackles allowed.

He winced as he sat, and I turned to the guard. "Unshackle his ankles."

"Can't do that Ma'am," he said.

"If you won't, then I will. He's in a leg brace, he isn't running anywhere." I stood and held out my hand for the keys.

The guard heaved a sigh and bent to undo the lock. Taggart relaxed as he stretched the injured leg out in front of him. When the guard moved to stand sentinel by the door, I waved him out. "I'll be fine, Officer."

"Whatever you say, Detective."

"Ezri Trenton, to what do I owe this particular early morning disturbance?" Taggart said, his voice distorted by the damage to his nasal cavity.

"Oh, you know, I wanted to take a trip down memory lane with my favorite murderous ex-FBI agent."

He leaned forward, but I caught the wince as he did so. If I had to guess, he had some bruised ribs under those prison blues. The fact he knew my name and gave me his usual look of disdain at least confirmed he still possessed his memories. "You only ever come here when you want something."

"Well, it's not like we're prison pen pals. And as it happens, I do need something from you." I lowered my voice. "I need you to throw me into that wall."

"I can assure you despite the evidence to the contrary, I

have not recently suffered head trauma. I have no desire to end up in solitary confinement."

"I don't need you to lay a hand on me. I just need to confirm something." Moreover, solitary confinement might be safer for him if the death creature really was starting to pick off Order members. Then again, given its appearance in my back seat, maybe not.

"What are you playing at, Savior?"

"Funny you should mention that word. In case it's news to you, I've got another prophecy hanging over my head that your Order buddies aren't too keen on me averting."

"You do have a nasty habit of getting in the way of such carefully laid plans."

"And surviving stabbings?" I quipped.

"For argument's sake, let's assume I do know that there is something brewing that you might hypothetically be involved in. What on earth makes you think I'm going to throw you across this room?"

I pointed toward the door. "We both know that he'll never know. And it's to prove a point. Now, am I going to have to make the first move so you can claim self-defense or are you going to grow some balls and just do it?"

The room grew thick with the scent of garlic, although it wasn't nearly as rotten as it had been when he was controlling Kevin months ago. Before my own power could react, I was on my feet and pinned to the wall opposite him. My chest constricted and I fought to breathe. As instinct took over and my arms flailed on autopilot, I realized that he'd called upon the bit of his magic I carried within me. He was turning it against me, willing it to encase me in stone.

"Point proven. Back down before I make you," I ground out, the smell of strawberries cascading off me in waves, forcing the magic down and back into its dormant state.

Taggart slumped against the chair when my feet were planted on the ground again. He hadn't used his magic in a while if it had worn him out that much. He took a few deep, if ragged, breaths to regain his composure. "And what point were we just proving?"

"That you still have your magic."

His brow furrowed which seemed unnecessary, the gesture being quite painful given the injury to his nose. "Why wouldn't I still have it?"

"Because your buddy Reuben Wickham somehow succeeded in raising that death creature and it's going around ripping magic away from members of the Order. Not that I care about bad guys no longer being a threat to the good, law-abiding practitioners in this city, but I'm not thrilled about it amassing power."

"They managed it?" He murmured.

"Bringing back Bearach's death manifestation from eight hundred years ago? Yeah, they did. Now you're going to tell me why and what it wants."

He looked at me with watery eyes, so unlike the man who'd strode into the precinct nearly a year ago and acted like *he* was the savior of all our problems. "You really expect me to have insight into activities that have taken place since my incarceration? As I told you at our last meeting, I have no information to give. I have cut ties with them."

"So, you haven't seen Dominic Janty or Reuben Wickham since you've been locked up?"

"Much to your chagrin I have not. We associated for a purpose, but that doesn't mean I liked them or enjoyed spending time with them. It was more of a mutually benefi-cial arrangement than any sort of friendship."

"Whose idea was it to try and bring back the druids in the first place?"

"You'd love it to be mine, wouldn't you?" He scoffed.

"Frankly, I wouldn't be surprised. But the more I dig into the Order, the more I'm beginning to see you don't actually have a real figurehead. You all like to talk a big game about being in charge and having power. Yet all you've done is manipulate other people into hurting others and what has it gotten you? A life sentence in a place where everyone else wants you dead. And Wickham doesn't even remember he ever had magic."

"That's not possible."

I leaned back in the chair and propped my hands behind my head. "Oh, it most definitely is. His magic is gone completely. There's nothing left of it. The memory of ever knowing it existed has been stripped from his mind. He thinks he was in a car accident that affected his memory."

"And you believe the creature they resurrected is responsible?"

"Let's just say a few months back I took a trip that was very illuminating, and I saw some pretty messed up shit that wants to hurt me. So yeah, I think it did and I don't think it's done."

"I don't know what else I can tell you. You were present when the spell to bring them back failed. You stopped it."

"Well someone managed to bring back some creepy, faceless incarnation of death created by some madman centuries ago."

"Wickham was the one obsessed with the history and origins of magic in the region. As you've no doubt learned, both sides of our feud come from Ireland."

"Oh yeah, I got up close and personal with Aoife and Bearach ... even saw how he nearly snuffed out light magic and took control over his coven by murdering his boss. I guess if this thing was created out of that bloodlust, it makes sense it would start taking the strongest dark magic it could find."

His gaze flickered to the door and he kneaded his hands as much as the shackles on his wrists would allow. "To be honest, I thought the latest beating was provoked by some new inmates, but you are right that there are certain members with more influence and sway over the organization."

"Did these new cellmates of yours happen to sport a particular brand?"

"Even if they did, I am stronger than flunkies. But I hadn't considered they were trying to take me out."

"Janty's worried he's next."

"He was Wickham's right hand."

Interesting.

"If you'd succeeded back in March and brought back these druids, what did you expect to happen? That they'd somehow decide to listen to you, because they were so grateful to you for bringing them back to a world they know nothing about?"

"Something like that," he sighed.

I leaned forward again. "I don't get you, Taggart. You were one of us. You went into law enforcement, a part of you had to have wanted to help people at least in the beginning. Anarchists don't generally join up with organized government entities. Or did you not have as much clout as you want people to believe?"

"I told you, I wanted freedom to use my abilities as I saw fit. If that happened to be stopping a drug dealer or something like that, so be it. We aren't anarchists. We don't want chaos. We want freedom to live and practice as we please. We don't want arbitrary rules forced on us."

"And look where that pursuit of freedom got you."

He'd given me another angle with Janty to explore. That was all I was likely to get out of him.

"Enjoy your time in here, Taggart. Try not to die."

I started toward the door when he reached out. His magic looped around my wrist, stopping my forward momentum. "This new prophecy. What does it say?"

I pivoted to face him. "Why do you care?"

"Just tell me. I answered your questions, the least you could do is answer one of mine."

"That when dark magic is at its height and Death's child reigns, the last of Harrow's blood will flow forevermore or else all light magic is doomed. I'm paraphrasing the last bit, but you get the gist."

His face fell. "There shouldn't have been a way for you to survive what I did to you, not even with the best Healers in the world, and yet, you did. I see now why."

"Because I'm a badass?" I offered with a smirk.

"Because the world wasn't done with you yet. Guess times have changed." His expression softened. "I'm almost sorry for what's coming for you. You were young and inexperienced. Yet, you've proven yourself to be stronger than any of us ever gave you credit for."

"People have a habit of underestimating me."

"I hope you're not one of those people. Because you do realize if you don't fulfill this prophecy, not just the people you love are going to be hurt. Everyone, everywhere is going to be in danger."

I pressed one hand to my chest. "I didn't know you cared."

"It's an unimaginable burden to place on one person. It seems magic has decided neither of us deserves freedom. Don't forget that darkness is stronger at this time."

"It's hard to forget", I retorted and knocked on the door for the guard to escort me out.

I left the visitation room behind me and I spotted a familiar face coming toward me down the hall. Kayla looked surprised to see me. Her dark purple pixie cut was a little longer these days, but her mostly black outfit remained the same. For a moment I wondered if she was stuck in that outfit permanently since she essentially became invisible thanks to her magic turning her into a Whisperer.

"Do I even want to know what you're doing here?" Kayla asked, peering over my shoulder as the guard ushered Taggart back to his cell.

"A case. Desmond's case," I replied.

"We all miss him," she said, looking downward. She'd been his eyes and ears when we'd first met. I'd almost forgotten she was processing his loss, too.

I gestured toward the visitation room behind me. "You here to see Kevin?"

"Yeah. He's doing better these days. He asks about you sometimes."

"Tell him I said hi and that I've been thinking of him," I said and gave her a quick pat on the shoulder before heading to reclaim my badge, gun, and phone.

When I had just repositioned the holster and turned my phone back on I saw several missed calls from Tricia along with a voicemail.

I pressed the phone to my ear as I headed to the car. "Ezri, it's Tricia. I know it's early, sorry, but I needed you to know something. After you stopped by, I took another look at the bullet from Desmond's case. I don't know how I missed it before. You need to get to the lab, now."

I didn't stop to figure out if she'd called Jacquie, too. I just got in the car and drove. The Medical Examiner's office was slow, not surprising for the early morning hour, as I pulled into the parking lot and jogged inside. I found Tricia pacing back and forth in front of the equipment in the lab.

"What did you find?" I blurted before the door could close behind me.

She looked up at my entry and shook her head. "I don't know why you get all the cases with the unexplainable evidence, but ... just look."

She pointed to the screen of the computer behind her. I studied the swirl of a partial fingerprint. "It's a partial print."

"On the bullet they took from Desmond," she said. "I don't know how I missed it before. I swear I examined it thoroughly and didn't see it before. But then I just got this feeling that I should look again and there it was."

"You haven't by chance run into a hipster chick with blonde hair, glasses and perpetually wearing headphones, have you? Or noted the smell of cinnamon somewhere it didn't make sense?" I told Avery not to do anything illegal, but nudging the ME along sounded right up her alley.

She wrinkled her nose. "What? No." After a beat, she continued. "I found the print and ran it through the database, not expecting a hit honestly. I mean, it would mean whoever shot Desmond wasn't wearing gloves when they loaded the gun. But then it found something."

I tried to temper my excitement. "Was you realizing you missed the partial print the weird thing, because I agree, you are usually way more thorough than that."

"I'm going to ignore that dig, because I kind of deserve it. No, the weird thing is it came up with a possible match. Except the match doesn't make sense, because it belongs to a deceased victim from a past case of yours."

"What case?"

She tapped a few keys and a photo of Adrian came up on the screen. "You're right that doesn't make sense, because he was very much dead ... way before Desmond was shot."

"We confirmed it with dental records, because of the fire damage."

An uneasy thought occurred to me. "Are you sure it's him and not a relative? I mean, both of his parents are still alive." Could Belladonna have acted out from her own grief?

"It is only a partial print so it's possible the system got it wrong and it's actually a familial match. That would be more plausible."

More plausible, yes, but it doesn't explain why one of Adrian's relatives would take out Desmond. Unless reason wasn't driving them. "Thanks for this. I need to follow up on it."

"I hope you catch whoever did this. I hate not being able to really close out the case, you know?"

More than you know.

"I do. Thank you for this, Tricia. I really appreciate it."

I had one foot out the door when she spoke again. "Spearmint."

"What?" I turned back to look at her.

"I don't know why you thought I smelled cinnamon, but it made me realize I think I remembered the scent of spearmint when I found the print. I was probably chewing gum and forgot or something."

"Yeah, maybe."

I managed to get back to the car before breaking down. The tears are hot against my cheeks as I rested my head against the steering wheel. I half expected Grandma to show up and tell me to stop being such a wuss, but no one came.

"Des, I hate you right now, you know that?" I say to the empty interior of the car. "I don't know what I did to make you so mad at me, but I'm trying to get answers. I want to put you to rest, because I know I can't face this thing without knowing what really happened. And I know you want me to come to realizations on my own, but haven't we found out that you keeping shit secret from me ends badly?"

Despite the anger starting to tighten my throat, a sense of relief warred for dominance. He's still out there in some form, guiding Tricia so she could point me in Adrian's direction.

Wiping my eyes with the back of my hand and taking a few sobering breaths, I pulled up Jacquie's number on my speed dial. I was about to hit 'Call' when her name flashed across the screen.

"I was just about to call you. We need to find Belladonna Montes."

"That's going to have to wait. Dominic Janty and two other people are being rushed to the hospital in comas after an apparent suicide pact."

I ARRIVED at the hospital and raced into the ER just as an ambulance came screaming in off the street. The driver climbed out, barreling to the back door and flinging it open.

"Dominic Janty, fifty-six-year-old male, intubated in the field, suspected drug overdose," the medic announced as his partner rolled the gurney out.

"J.T.?" I blurt as my fiancé appeared, one hand pumping oxygen into Janty's body.

"Ez, what are you doing here?" He moved into the ER proper and I followed after him.

"He's a suspect," I said vaguely.

"Well, we've got two more coming in behind us. I'll catch up with you later. And whatever this is, it better not interfere with our afternoon plans."

"Nothing is going to stop me from marrying you today," I called as he disappeared with Janty.

I ignored the bemused look from his partner and moved out of the flow of incoming traffic from the ambulance bay. Jacquie pulled me aside and we sat in a pair of chairs pressed up against a wall.

"So, what do we know about what happened to Janty?" I pressed; my own news forgotten.

"Just that it appeared he and two others ingested some sort of toxin."

I flashed back to when Lola Cox had tried to take her

own life using her magic, turning it against herself. I'd managed to get some answers out of her before she flatlined, but I didn't know if this was the same situation.

"Why do we need to find Belladonna?" Jacquie's voice drew me out of the memory.

"Tricia found a partial print on the bullet that killed Desmond and it's at least a familial match to Adrian."

"She told us two days ago she had nothing else in the way of evidence," she hissed.

I sighed. "It sounds like Desmond may have nudged her along or something. She mentioned smelling spearmint when she found the print. Maybe I'm reading into it too much, but it feels like he wants me to find the answer and not the easy way. Which, let's be real, is kind of Des to a T."

"That does sound like him," she agreed. "You don't really think Belladonna had something to do with it, do you?"

"I don't know. It would make more sense than her son who'd already been dead three months to do it."

Before Jacquie could respond, J.T. appeared at the other end of the ER. He weaved through nurses and doctors making rounds on patients. He stopped when he was standing less than six inches from me.

"They're trying to get him stable, but it doesn't look good."

The doors of the ambulance bay burst open and two more gurneys rolled through. I caught enough from the medics sharing information with the triage team to know it was our other two Order members.

"Do you think they turned their own magic against themselves, like Lola did?" I whispered.

"It's possible. My nose isn't as good as yours at picking

up magic when it's been used. But if you're right and that's what happened, why would they do that?'"

"Because they made the decision to not feed the beast," I muttered. "I need to know when he's at least stable."

"You aren't going to get anything from him," J.T. said.

"Not verbally, but there are other ways of communicating."

"He's going to be in a coma, Ez. He's not talking to you."

"I have had practice talking to people in comas," I reminded him. If I just went in by myself this time, there was less of a chance I'd destabilize his grip on life quite as quickly as I had with Lola.

"That's too dangerous. Besides, aren't you relieved there are three less Order members roaming around?'

I didn't want to argue with him. "While I'm happy there are less people luring kids to the Dark Side, that doesn't stop the death monster that's trying to rip apart the world. And Taggart all but confirmed that if it took Wickham's magic like I think it did, it's just getting stronger."

"You saw Taggart?" He demanded.

"Didn't I mention that?" He shook his head. *Oops.* "I had to know what he knew. Turns out, not as much as I hoped. The whole resurrecting the druids thing had been Wickham's brainchild. Guess that backfired on him in a big way."

"I still don't know how trying to talk to a coma patient is going to help you stop this thing," Jacquie said.

"I'm not sure it will, but I have to try. In the meantime, we try to track down our wayward mother. She and I are going to have a long chat." Assuming I don't get stuck in Janty's head, if and when he kicks the bucket.

"All of this saving the world better not get in the way of

our very important date this afternoon," J.T. said, pulling me to my feet and wrapping his arms around my waist.

"I will be there. I swear." Despite the fact we were standing in the middle of a busy hospital's ER, I kissed him and held on tight.

"If you two love birds are done, we'd better get going if you want to fit in all of these heroics before your vows," Jacquie prompted.

I pulled myself out of J.T.'s arms and followed Jacquie out of the hospital. Belladonna had fallen off the map since Desmond's death. I wasn't sure why I didn't connect it sooner. I just had to hope I could still hunt her down before time ran out.

THIRTEEN

"So where do we start?" Jacquie followed me out of the hospital and toward my car.

I hadn't stopped to ask how she'd ended up here or who'd even notified her about Janty and the others before. "How did you find out that they'd all tried to commit suicide? We don't have an active case with them ..." She arched a dark brow at me as my brain filled in the rest. "But Molly does, and she gave you the head's up."

"See, isn't it better when branches of law enforcement can work cooperatively," my partner replied.

"I hope this hasn't completely torpedoed her case."

"Sounded like there were more players involved than just Janty, so she's got enough leverage to keep her case moving. But you really think they tried to take the coward's way out rather than succumb to this monster they helped bring back?"

"Honestly, I wouldn't blame them if they did. This thing has been popping up in my head for months now and whenever it damn well wants. I can feel its power, even when it's not physically near me. I won't lie, it's scared me enough that I've considered whether I'm the right person to face it."

"Come on, let's go find Belladonna so your fiancé doesn't murder me for keeping his bride-to-be from getting to the altar on time."

"It's a clerk's desk at City Hall, but the sentiment is appreciated."

"Speaking of finding our missing mother, any thoughts on how to do that?" She repeated.

"Avery's less pissed at me today ... I think anyway. If anyone can track someone down, it's her."

I checked the clock on the dashboard of my car as we made the trip out to Authority Headquarters. If we didn't find Belladonna by noon, I'd have to put it off until the morning. I refused to let my friends and family down by missing my own wedding.

Entering the building didn't feel quite the same anymore, I'd been staying away, but even when I did come by, I half expected to see Desmond waiting for me. I shook off the wave of sadness as I left the meeting room behind, Jacquie right behind me and slipped into the tech hub. As I'd hoped, Avery sat there in front of the computers, fiddling with more photos of her and Desmond.

"Hey," I said and rapped my knuckles against the door-frame. Jacquie hung back, giving us privacy.

She spun in the chair to face me. Unlike when I'd shown up with video footage of her husband's murder, she looked less like she wanted to rip my head off. "Hey."

"I know I don't have any right to ask you this, but I need you to find someone for me."

"That's not really what I do," she replied.

"It's a lead and I think ... as weird as it sounds, Desmond sent it."

Her eyes widened behind her glasses and she slid the headphones off her neck. "What ... How?"

"I think he might have guided the medical examiner in finding some new evidence they'd missed before. It's a little thin, but we need to find Belladonna."

"She fell off the grid after Desmond died. Like she just took off, abandoning her seat on the Council."

"I figured as much. But, if digging into family history showed me anything, it's that she doesn't have much family left. She may not be in the city anymore, but we still have to look. If Des is giving us this clue, we have to follow it as far as it will take us."

Avery pivoted the chair to face the monitors again. "Let me get some other guys I know on this. Don't worry, we can trust them. How much of a time crunch are we working under?"

"Well, I'd kind of like to put this to rest before I have to fulfill another prophecy in less than twenty-four hours."

"As soon as fucking possible. Understood." I was about to leave her to her tech wizardry when she reached out and grabbed my hand. "I'm sorry ... I sort of lost my shit on you before."

"You had every right to hate me for what I made you do."

"You were looking for help anywhere you could, and I just let my grief get in the way of that."

"Avery, really, it's okay. We all miss him and what's done is done. I have to believe this new evidence came to light, because it's right up your alley."

She smiled, but it was merely a shadow of the ones I'd seen break out on her face when Des was alive. "You know, you've kind of got this whole hero thing down. Weirdly uplifting speeches and all."

"Thanks, I think."

In that moment, my phone blared with an obnoxiously sad tuba. J.T. had gotten hold of my phone, reverted to his stupid teenage-boy brain and messed with all my ringtones and alerts. I smiled in spite of myself and checked the message.

I looked at Jacquie over my shoulder. "Guess we're heading back to the hospital. They've stabilized Janty, but we won't have long. J.T.'s managed to persuade one of the nurses in the ICU that he's friends with to take a little longer on rounds."

"Go, be the hero." Avery waved me out of the room. As I descended the steps out of the building, I couldn't help, but wonder if this was one of the last times, I'd see this place.

WALKING BACK through the ER doors gave me a weird sense of déjà vu. I scanned the people waiting to be seen lining the hall we'd waited in earlier until I spotted J.T. He waved us toward a set of stairs and only once we were there did he speak.

"Carlotta is a friend from a long time ago. She doesn't know about magic per se, but she's sympathetic. Also, when I impressed on her that my police detective fiancée needed a little help, she jumped at the chance. He's upstairs on the second floor."

"I remember the way," I replied and led the way up.

The last time I'd made a similar trek, it had been in the middle of the night with Molly and I cloaked in Kayla's Whisperer invisibility. What I wouldn't have given to have some of that now. I didn't need people wondering why the police were going into his room. After all, Janty probably didn't know he was in the FBI's crosshairs.

I nudged open the door after getting a hit from the hand sanitizer outside—a girl couldn't be too careful—and stepped inside, leaving Jacquie to stand watch. I was about to address the unconscious man when I heard the squeak of shoes on the linoleum. I spun, hand moving on instinct to my gun, and my magic bubbled to the surface, ready to strike when Molly stepped out of the bathroom.

"Jeez, you nearly got yourself shot," I huffed.

"I figured you'd be showing up sooner or later to question him. He doesn't have any family to notify so no one was suspicious that I've been waiting." She glanced at the man in the bed. "I don't know that he's in much of a state to talk like this though."

"Same deal as with Lola," I said.

"You think you can try not to make him have a heart attack or whatever happened to her?"

"Can't make any promises. You have anything you want me to ask him about that might help your case? I figure turnabout's fair play."

"I appreciate the offer, but I think I've gotten all I can out of him. I'm guessing you don't want any passengers along for this ride."

"That would be correct." I glanced toward the chart hanging off the foot of the bed.

"He and the others have the medical staff baffled. No evidence of a toxin in their body, but they clearly all fell into comas at the same time."

"Definitely sounds like the Order's go-to move to keep their people quiet."

"Don't take too long, Ezri." She gave me a pat on the shoulder before stepping out of the room.

I could hear her exchanging pleasantries with Jacquie as I slid off my jacket and laid it across the back of the solitary chair in the corner. I unhooked my gun and set that in the chair as well. I didn't need him having some weird involuntary spasm, getting his hands on my weapon and getting off a shot.

Perching on the side of the bed, I took in his appearance. He'd been assured of himself at the bar only a few hours ago. Now, he looked frail, pallid and almost lifeless. The pillows and blankets appeared to have a brighter glow to them than he did. The machines beeped in steady rhythm, keeping him alive, even if his mind was already gone.

"Let's hope you're still in there," I whispered and took his hand.

I poured my own magic into his hand, letting it connect us. The beeping of the machines dimmed to my hearing and my vision tunneled so all I could see was him. It wasn't as jarring this time as it had been with Lola. I tried to file that away for later contemplation as the hospital room faded away, replaced by a dim grey void. Janty stood at the center of it and he looked ... *relieved* to see me?

"You were expecting me?" I asked, my voice muted by the surroundings.

"I had hoped it just wouldn't be what I expect is trying to come for us all in the dark."

"I've met your monster and it's nasty. But maybe there's still time to return it to the pet store?"

Janty laughed. "You're so young. No, there is nothing that we can do to banish it. It has a foothold here now. We're just pawns in its game."

"And what does this thing want? World domination? Ultimate power?"

"All of the above?" He quipped with a shrug. "I don't envy you, Savior. What a funny thing to have need of one in these modern times."

"Believe me I didn't ask for this. I was born to it." Literally. "If you can't put this creepy genie back in the bottle, you have any thoughts on how I can stop it?"

"Don't mistake our discussion here for me switching sides. I still believe in the Order's mission."

"So does your buddy Taggart, rotting away in prison for following the Order's mission. You all claim you want freedom to practice magic how you see fit and yet it always seems to bite you in the ass. There can't be chaos in the world. It just doesn't work. There has to be some rules."

Our surroundings began to grow dimmer and I felt an icy chill run down my neck. I watched Janty react to the same sensation and he tried to take a step backward, but there was nowhere to go. The void of his mind was endless and yet it was keeping us right here, immobile.

"Look, we both know you aren't long for this world. There's very little chance I'm going to blab to your besties that you told me the secret to defeating the very thing that you killed yourself to get away from." I noted.

"You can't defeat it. Not alone. You aren't powerful enough. It would take more magic than any one person possesses."

"You believe you could escape me," that damn creepy voice rasped all around us.

"Not that I want you to get Dementored or whatever is about to happen, but I'm not sticking around for it," I said.

"You can't leave me here with that thing!" Janty protested.

"You made your bed, Janty. Now you've got to lay in it. I am sorry about all of this. I wish it didn't have to end this way, but you're the one responsible for bringing this thing back."

I turned my attention to breaking the bond between us. I didn't need the death creature trying to suck away my magic, too. The hospital room came flooding back into view and I yanked my hand free of Janty as he began to convulse in the bed. I could pick up a hint of his magic hanging in the air for a few seconds. I swore it shimmered above his body before disappearing with a soft 'pop.' I would have expected the scent to linger longer, but it simply vanished. Taking a cleansing hit from the sandalwood around my neck, I concentrated, but the signature was truly gone. He'd been who knows how far from that thing and yet it had still managed to steal his power.

I repressed the urge to vomit and grabbed my gun and jacket before backing out of the room. The monitors weren't blaring yet, but I suspected they would be soon. Janty had tried to kill himself to keep his power safe and that had failed. Even if he managed to survive, he would be left with no idea why he would have tried to end his life. Jacquie and Molly both waited across the hall. I didn't speak, just headed straight for the stairwell, descending to the first floor in silence.

"What happened? Did you get answers?" Molly demanded, barring my way out of the stairwell.

"I don't know. He was talking in circles. He seemed to think I can't defeat this thing by myself. Except, that's exactly what the prophecy is saying. I am the only one that can stop it. And then that thing showed up. I watched it take his magic. It was there one second and then it just didn't exist anymore."

Before Molly could ask any more questions, Jacquie's phone beeped with an incoming text message. She studied it, glanced at me and then at Molly. "Hate to cut this short, but we have somewhere to be."

Molly led the way out of the stairwell and into the main part of the hospital. The sudden change of lighting made my eyes ache and I squinted against the brightness of the hallway. Jacquie pressed a firm hand to the small of my back and guided me out of the hospital.

"Where are we going?" I could only get the words out once we were in her car. I'd have to come back for mine. "Is there a new lead on the case?"

She gave me side-eye and shook her head. "Not about the case. You'll see."

I didn't like it when my partner was vague with me. It rarely boded well and given that we had a creepy magic-stealing monster on the loose, it worried me even more as she pulled out into traffic.

FOURTEEN

I spotted the precinct as we whizzed past, leaving it far behind. We trailed the green line of the transit system moving north of the city, finally pulling into a courthouse I hadn't been to before.

"Jacquie, can you please tell me what's going on?"

"You'll find out soon enough." Jacquie said.

I had no choice, but to follow as she marched across the street. When we reached the front steps, I moved to bar her path forward.

"Can you please tell me what the hell is going on?" I repeated when she offered no other explanation.

"You're the one who insisted on getting married today," she replied as if that should give me all the answers I needed.

"Yeah, at City Hall." I gestured back the way we'd come. "Not here."

She gripped me by the shoulders and spun me around, giving me a shove up the first step or two. I caught my balance just as the door opened and J.T. stepped out, his coat half zipped. "Good, you made it."

I closed the distance between us, glaring at my partner one last time before stepping into the warmth of the courthouse entryway. "Want to tell me what we're doing here?'

"Well, I realized after we decided to do this whole marriage thing without a ton of planning that there was a waiting period of three days. Given that we want to do this before you have to face down unimaginable horrors of dark magic tomorrow, we have to get a waiver," he explained.

I blinked at him, the mundane nature of his words settling over me. I'd been so focused on everything magical around me. I hadn't even stopped to think about the little things like making sure we had a valid marriage license or rings. At least we had our vows already. The fact that he'd anticipated my lack of attention to that particular detail made me all the happier to know I'd soon get to call him husband.

"One more thing," Jacquie said and stepped just inside the doors beside me. Without asking permission, she unholstered my gun and freed it from my belt.

She didn't need to explain the reason. I knew the hassle of having to secure my weapon before going into court. I flashed a grateful smile before J.T. led me by the hand into the security line. It moved quickly and J.T. guided me to the floor we needed for Probate and Family Court. We stopped just outside the Clerk's Office and J.T. produced an already filled out waiver form, minus our signatures.

"I love you," I proclaimed and pulled him in for a kiss. I didn't care who saw me. I'd pushed him away for too long and I was starting to think I might be risking our future together to face down this prophecy.

My body tingled as we walked inside and got in line. I checked my phone, ostensibly to make sure we didn't run late to our own wedding ceremony. I also hoped Avery would have gotten back to me with something on Belladonna's location.

Nothing.

"Were you able to talk to that guy?" J.T. whispered as we shuffled forward in line.

"I'll fill you in later. This is more important," I replied, squeezing his right hand with my left, making sure he felt the weight of the engagement ring on my finger.

"Next," the clerk called, and we stepped up to the counter.

The man with a receding hairline and glasses secured around his neck on a thin silver chain watched as we signed the waiver and presented it. He studied it and then looked at us.

"And when were you planning to get married?"

"This afternoon," we chimed in unison.

"And the reason you are seeking the waiver?"

My mouth went dry. I'd just assumed we would present the form; the clerk would notarize it and we'd be good to go. I hadn't realized we needed more than that. I glanced sideways at J.T. and he looked as surprised by the question as me. At least we'd been on the same page.

"Health reasons," I finally said.

He gave me another look, sighed, and pulled out a notary stamp, affixing it to our waiver form. "Good luck."

I snatched the paper from him before he could change his mind and decide we didn't deserve to get out of waiting to get married. Having the waiver in hand together we wound our way back to the door we'd come through.

"So, we're really doing this," J.T. said, slinging his arm around my shoulder.

Yeah, we are.

The realization that my life was about to change for the

better in a way magic could never replicate crashed into me like a wave. It left me excited and at once saddened that my mother wasn't here to see it. Not in the way that other relatives who'd passed could be. I had no doubt Grandma would put in an appearance.

"Hey, talk to me," J.T. whispered, ushering me to a vacant bench down the hall.

"Sorry, it's just hitting me that my mom won't be here for this."

He took my chin in his hand and tilted my head up to meet his gaze. He brushed the tears away with his thumb and kissed me gently on the lips. "I know you wanted her to be here for this. I know we both wanted Des to be here, but life had other plans. That doesn't mean they aren't still with us in spirit."

I touched the pendant at my throat. "Except I have relatives who literally can be here in spirit and neither of them are among them. I know you're trying to cheer me up and I appreciate it, truly I do. I think I just need to sit on this for a minute."

"Whatever you need." He kissed me again and sat beside me in stoic silence.

Magic had been a great gift, letting me do amazing things that most people could only dream of. Although it had taken so much from me, too, without considering how I felt about it. I knew it was selfish to think magic owed me after all I'd been through, but it didn't stop the thought from flickering across my consciousness.

"There's still time to make it do what you want," a gravelly voice echoed in my mind.

I wasn't going to let that thing get in my head, not about this. I turned my focus inward, building up a mental wall, brick by strawberry-tinged brick until there was no room for that creature inside. I should have done it sooner. I might have slept better and doubted myself less.

"So, are you ready to be Mrs. Somers?" J.T. broke through my mental fortification.

I snorted. "You know I'm not changing my name. Besides, Mrs. Somers will always be your mom," I quipped and stood, pulling him with me.

"Fair point."

I rejoined Jacquie as we headed to City Hall, leaving J.T. to get there on his own. I fiddled with the ring on my finger and as the cityscape whizzed by, I let myself drift off in thought. Back before my mother's death, I'd dreamed of marrying J.T. He'd been my first love. After I'd ex-communicated myself from the Authority and everyone associated with magic, I never thought we'd be back in each other's lives ... let alone about to say "I do." He'd waited for me and in a way, I'd waited for him, too. I'd been so focused on my career; I hadn't given myself time to date. Maybe, subconsciously, I'd been holding out hope we'd reconnect.

As Jacquie pulled into a parking spot, my phone pinged with a new email message. It was a single line of text, reading 'Congratulations. She'd be proud.' from Iain Nobles. I suppose an email was cheaper than an international call from Ireland. I suspected J.T. had passed on the information. We'd only spent a short time in each other's presence, but Iain had changed the course of my future. I appreciated the well wishes and smiled at the gesture.

Standing in the bathroom of City Hall twenty minutes later, tugging on a three-quarter length sleeve dress in the middle of winter seemed a little stupid. Despite that I wasn't that much into bucking the trend to not at least wear a dress to my own wedding.

"You know she's with you, even if you can't feel her," Grandma said, sitting on the sink to my right, kicking her legs back and forth like a child.

"I know, Grandma."

'You look very pretty," she complimented as I shivered.

"Good thing I don't have to spend long in it."

Grandma gave me a feigned look of horror. "Say it ain't so, my little Ezzie making sexy jokes?"

I rolled my eyes. "Not what I meant, and you know it, seeing as you apparently live in my head. Now, can you please behave? I don't need to get weird looks from the magistrate."

She reached over and cupped my cheek. "For you, I think I can manage."

"You almost ready in there?" Jacquie called from just outside the door.

I checked myself in the mirror one last time. "Guess that's my cue."

The relative safety of the bathroom left me unprepared for the whirlwind of emotions that hit me as I walked into the small chapel space. J.T. stood at the far end, his parents beside him. Dad sat in one of the back rows, hands clasped tight in his lap. Jacquie tapped him on the shoulder, and he stood, stumbling over himself in his bid to get to me.

"You look beautiful," he whispered and kissed my cheek.

"Thanks, Dad."

Jacquie moved around the perimeter of the space, ready to take up her spot on my side of the magistrate. She'd changed into a knee length burgundy dress with matching jewelry. I blinked back tears and Grandma stood just to Jacquie's left. She gave me a nod and stowed her aviators in her front pocket.

"Grandma's here," I whispered back to my dad as he looped his arm through mine. I did my best to gesture discreetly to where Grandma stood, invisible to the rest of the people around us.

"See, your mom's side of the family is represented after all," Dad commented with a small smile. He kept his gaze focused ahead of him as he led me down the aisle.

My mouth went dry as he stopped and offered J.T. a firm handshake before leaning in to whisper something in his ear. Next, he pivoted to kiss me on the cheek one last time and join Jacquie behind me.

"If you two would like to join hands," the magistrate said, her tone a low alto that somehow filled me with a sense of calm I would have normally attributed to magic.

Yet, as I inhaled and took J.T.'s hands, I couldn't sense any sort of magical signal boost. She was mundane, perfectly mundane. Swallowing in quick succession in the hopes of regaining my ability to speak when it came time, I watched as the magistrate turned first to J.T.

"Are you ready?'

He beamed at me and gave my hands a squeeze. "I hope so."

"It's my understanding you've chosen to use prepared vows," the magistrate said and nodded to J.T. "Once you've said them, we'll do the exchange of rings, then the kiss, and you'll be married."

J.T. nodded again and cleared his throat. "Ez, you've been the love of my life for the last twelve years, since that first day you walked into my life. I knew you were special, and it wasn't because of the expectations other people placed on you. You were the girl I wanted to spend the rest of my life with, however long that may be." He paused to wipe his eyes with the back of his hand, strands of hair falling across his face.

"I knew it wasn't going to be an easy road and it took us a long time to get here. But there is nowhere else I'd rather be standing right now than here with you, promising to love you for the rest of our days. You continue to amaze me every day and I can't wait to see what else is coming our way."

My own tears flowed freely as he finished speaking. *How am I supposed to follow that?* He reached over and wiped my cheeks again with the pads of his thumbs. I leaned into them, letting his touch ground me.

"J.T., I don't deserve you," I began. "But you've seen me at my worst, and you waited for me to get my head out of my ... well, you know, and see what was right in front of me. The man who has that much patience should be a saint and I can't think of anyone more deserving of that title than you. You make me want to be the best version of myself. You make me smile and laugh at your corny jokes."

Out of the corner of my eye I caught Grandma snickering into her hand even though no one else could see or hear her. Jacquie even cracked a smirk and Dad blushed. J.T.'s parents just stood side-by-side with grins on their faces.

"I can't wait to spend the rest of my life with you. Learning to be better and knowing that you'll be there to remind me that this world doesn't have to be faced alone, no matter what I might think."

J.T. nodded in silence and I caught the slight motion as he shifted his weight forward, stopping himself from coming in for the kiss too soon. I ripped my gaze from his face to look at the magistrate.

"Well, those were certainly some of the more unique

vows I've heard in a while." She smiled at us and looked to Jacquie. "Do you have the rings?"

Jacquie stepped up and offered up the rings to the magistrate who cupped them delicately in her palms. They were simple bands to go with the one I already had. She passed one to J.T.

"Repeat after me," she said and began reciting the exchange of rings. J.T. followed suit.

"I, Jared Tyler, take you, Ezri, to be my wife. And with this ring, I bind us together in sickness and health, for better or worse, until death parts us." He slid the ring onto my finger, clinking it against the one already sitting there.

I studied the two bands stacked one on top of the other for a moment. It was such a simple action, putting a ring on someone's finger and yet it carried so much weight. No matter what happened next, I would be linked to him forever.

The magistrate handed me the ring for J.T. and I looked him in the eye. His left hand trembled as I took it in mine.

"I, Ezri, take you, Jared Tyler, to be my husband. And with this ring, I bind us together in sickness and health, for better or worse, until death parts us." *And beyond.*

As I slid the ring onto his finger, I let out a little hint of my magic, letting it slither around the bands on our fingers, coating them in strawberry, almost like tying a knot. The sweet scent of honey drenched over us and I could feel the bond strengthen as his magic joined with mine. It was subtle enough that our mundane magistrate wouldn't notice, but those with power in the room would understand the significance.

"By the power vested in me by the Commonwealth of Massachusetts, I pronounce you husband and wife. You may now kiss the bride."

J.T. pulled me to him and I felt the ethereal weight of his magic wrap around me just as he wrapped his arms loosely around my waist, kissing me. It wasn't the most chaste of kisses, but it wasn't as over the top as it could have been either, given our audience. My own magic rose up to greet his, marking him as my own.

I hadn't expected either of our magics to react like that, but it made sense. Our power was a part of us, rooted deep down in our DNA. The joining of our families should result in something new, a strengthening of our power. I wondered if whenever he used his magic now, if it would carry the barest hint of mine and vice versa.

I looked over as he dipped me and spotted Grandma wiping away ghostly tears from her cheeks before securing her aviators and disappearing. The pendant around my neck warmed, as if she was reminding me that she wasn't far away if I needed her.

J.T. let me up and I turned, throwing myself into Dad's waiting arms. "Congratulations, sweetheart."

"Thank you."

My new in-laws swooped in next, each giving me a firm squeeze and a kiss on the cheek before descending on J.T., leaving me with Jacquie. She looked proud.

"What's that look for?" I brushed strands of red out of my eyes, using it as an excuse to ogle my new bling.

"When I found out I was being partnered with you, I thought I knew what I was getting into. Desmond warned me you were headstrong and didn't want help from anyone."

"Thanks ... I think."

"And I knew you were young, but you've grown more than I would have thought possible in these last nine months, Ezri. And I'm proud of the woman you've become

... Of the detective you've become. You command the respect of those around you and that's not something everyone could do at your age."

"I'm glad you were here today," I said and fussed with the cuff on my right sleeve.

"We're family. Maybe not by blood or by magic, but I know you'd do anything to protect me and mine, and I'd do the same for you. That means something. Besides, it wasn't like I had any plans this afternoon," she quipped in a rare bit of sarcasm.

I didn't want to say that this felt like some sort of goodbye. I wasn't ready to accept that as a potential outcome, no matter what the signs were trying to tell me. I needed to hold on to the idea that I would be coming home to my husband and my friends tomorrow—with the world righted and the bad guys well and truly beaten. Even if it's just for a little while.

"Are you two coming? It wouldn't be a wedding without a party," J.T. called from the other end of the chapel.

"Don't keep your husband waiting," Jacquie said, making a shooing motion.

For a little while, we could revel in the joy of our marriage and I was ready to do just that.

FIFTEEN

We crammed into the back area of a tapas place that J.T. had insisted we try down near Coolidge Corner. The drinks were heavy on the alcohol and the charcuterie was sufficiently salty to keep me going back for more. It all felt so *normal*, sitting here as a family, laughing and sharing stories like it was just another night out.

Beside me, J.T. leaned in, kissing me unexpectedly on the cheek. I had a hunch it was the second margarita that had emboldened him, but no one seemed to notice or care. We were newlyweds and had license to be overly affectionate as the waiter came by with another round of tiny plates filled with far too small portions. I was grateful our parents had insisted on footing the bill for this.

"Hey, you felt it earlier, right?" J.T. said vaguely, pulling me in close so he didn't have to shout.

"If you mean the magic, yeah," I answered. I could still feel his magic lingering on my skin. I didn't dare take a hit from the sandalwood charm. I didn't want to wash it off. Not yet anyway. "Did you know that was going to happen?"

He shook his head. "No clue. I guess our parents wouldn't have had that, since our dads are mundane."

I nodded in understanding. I could have asked a relative like Theodora, but honestly, the thought hadn't occurred to me. Besides I wasn't in the habit of asking for romance advice from people who had lived several hundred years ago where they didn't believe in co-habitation and premarital sex.

"Why do I get the feeling you're not all here," he said and tugged me out of the booth.

I waited to answer until we stood out on the porch watching the cars and the occasional train trundle by outside. It wasn't exactly quiet, but it was far enough from the din inside that we wouldn't have to shout.

"I don't mean to be distracted. I'm loving just celebrating with you and our parents. I don't know why you never suggested this place before, because the food is amazing," I rambled. "I just can't keep tomorrow out of my head, even though I'm trying."

His expression clouded with sadness and maybe even a hint of fear. "I've been trying not to think about it either, but it's kind of hard to avoid a prophecy portending the end of days with only the woman I love standing up against evil winning."

I wrapped my arms around his neck. "You know there's no chance I'd let that happen if I had any say in the matter, right?"

"I know and I think that's part of what makes me afraid." He kissed me slow and soft on the lips. "We're just starting this new part of our lives together and what if ..."

"What if it means I don't come home to you?" I finished.

J.T. sighed. "I'm crazy, right, for thinking that?"

"No, you're not. Because I'm scared that might be what it means, too. Everyone keeps telling me this creature is stronger than me, that my magic won't be able to defeat it. But Aoife insists that I was put on this earth to rein this thing back in, to fix her mistakes. So, they can't both be true."

"I'll never be ready to lose you."

"Believe me, I don't want to lose you either." I studied his face, committing every contour and shadow to memory. The way he watched me like he was doing the same imprinted in my memory. "Let's promise each other that tonight is just for us. No prophecy, no world ending. Just you and me. Whatever happens tomorrow, that's for tomorrow."

"I think I can do that," he agreed just as Dad lumbered out.

"You two going to run off on us before dessert? They're bringing churros!"

"We'll be right in," I answered with a smile.

How was I going to possibly say goodbye to my dad if this prophecy was going to make me pay for an entire world's worth of mistakes? Had he gotten the chance to at least say goodbye to mom? I couldn't keep that chance from him now.

"Just give me one minute," I told J.T. and gestured to my dad.

Without words, he understood and kissed my cheek. He clapped my dad on the shoulder as he passed him by. Dad came to stand beside me on the porch. His shoulders tensed as he looked at me, maybe reading the anxiety in my own body language.

"Did you know before Mom did what she did?"

"I knew what she was going to try and do, yes."

"Did you know it would mean losing your wife?'

"It was a possibility." He wouldn't meet my gaze.

"Did you ever think about stopping her?'

"When you're a parent, you'll do anything to keep your children safe. Of course, I didn't want to lose the love of my life, but I knew even if I wasn't truly a part of your world that you needed to be kept safe as long as possible. I didn't expect it would have cost me my daughter, too."

"I wish I could make it up to you," I sighed and leaned into him, taking in the scent of him, clinging to the feel of his shoulder beneath my cheek.

"This sounds like a goodbye, Ezri."

"It's not. Not exactly. This thing that's waiting for me, it's big. Bigger than anything I've faced before. I hope it doesn't mean we have to say goodbye," I trailed off.

"But in case it does, you want to get it in before you go."

"Is that terrible?" I blinked up at him.

"No, sweetheart, it's not. Thank you."

We stood there for a few minutes longer before I took his hand in mine and weaved our way back to the party. J.T. embraced me with open arms and another flirty kiss. I let myself be buoyed by the happiness in the space around me. It was almost as fortifying as magic.

"You two need to have your first dance!" J.T.'s mom announced as a slow song blared over the speaker system. Why did I get the feeling she'd slipped the waiter some extra cash to mess with the playlist?

I groaned, but J.T. pulled me to my feet and we swayed along to the beat. I was grateful for the privacy, so we didn't get weird looks from other diners. The movement and the drinks made me light-headed as the lights sparkled and blurred around me.

The music faded and I felt a chill dance down my spine

and settle in my belly. I blinked against the sudden darkness as the restaurant disappeared.

"No. You do not get to take this night from me," I growled.

"You have rebuffed my offers of leniency. And you thought your meager defenses would keep me out, foolish Savior." The creature's voice hissed, its breath tickling the nape of my neck.

I swallowed back the bile rising in my throat. I refused to turn and face it. I wouldn't give it any more power than it already had. Not satisfied with that, it cackled, and the darkness gave way to an open stretch of snow-covered grass. I spotted the pathways of the Common crisscrossing the patches of grass. Bodies lined the space wearing the faces of my loved ones and friends. In the distance I could see another row of figures. Yet, unlike the creature taunting me, they didn't bring fear. They were my last line of defense.

"Your failure will mean their death. I will claim them all, magic-born or not. It matters not to me."

"You will not touch them. Now, get the fuck out of my head."

Honey-tinged strawberry erupted like a geyser from within my chest, wrapping J.T. and I in a protective bubble. The creature's presence receded. I pushed the bubble farther, letting it expand to cover our parents and Jacquie. I only relaxed when the chill vanished, and the room came back into focus.

J.T. watched me with worried eyes. "What happened?"

"A party crasher, but I took care of it," I answered.

J.T. glanced over his shoulder at the people sitting around the table watching us. *Were they any the wiser to what I'd done?* The music ended and we retreated to the table just as the waiter brought out metal cups filled with thick doughy, cinnamon-covered churros. I couldn't help thinking of the scent of Avery's magic and wondering if the hint of spearmint that had flavored Desmond's power had seeped into her signature as well.

"Do you want to get out of here?" J.T. whispered in my ear as I brushed cinnamon dust from my fingers.

"Is it rude to just bail on our own reception?"

"It's our wedding. I think they'll understand." He cleared his throat. "We wanted to just thank you guys so much for celebrating with us tonight ... and for picking up the tab. But, if there are no objections, we'd like to head home."

Dad flagged down our waiter and passed over a credit card while J.T. fumbled with requesting a car from one of the ride-share apps on his phone. Jacquie donned her coat and I trailed her to the door. "Thanks again for being a part of this."

"I'll see you tomorrow, partner."

"Hey, I know you've got my back, but something tells me that what's coming tomorrow is something I have to do by myself."

She looked at me and for a moment I caught sadness in her expression. "If you're sure."

I nodded and she left me standing there alone. J.T. stepped up beside me, wrapping his arms around me. "What really happened during that dance?" He breathed in my ear.

"It was trying to scare me by promising to hurt everyone I love."

"Let it try," he said.

"It won't get the chance. I have to go alone."

"No, we're not starting this again," he argued.

I spun to face him. "Maybe it was showing me what's to

come, maybe not. But I know that I wasn't really alone there." I tapped the pendant. "I've got their magic, too. I can do this. Please, let me protect you."

I could read his face, obviously he didn't like the idea. Though he nodded his understanding. With the fun over and the quiet of our condo waiting for us, I let myself hope that tomorrow wouldn't cost me everything I'd worked so hard to build.

DECEMBER 21, 2017

My phone buzzing its way off the nightstand and clattering to the floor was not how I pictured waking up to my first day as a married woman. I groaned, the haze of too much alcohol and food making my body heavy. J.T. lay beside me, one arm thrown over his head, his bare chest rising and falling as the blankets shifted with my movements.

I wasn't too hung over to remember the fun we'd had last night when we'd gotten home, keeping the promise to each other to celebrate and focus only on each other until morning. Well ... way into the morning. I groped blindly until my fingers found the charger cord, still miraculously plugged in. I tugged until I got my hand around the phone to see two missed calls and a text from Avery. I ignored them all and hit redial, pressing the phone to my ear and rolling over so that hopefully the sound wouldn't wake J.T.

"Finally," Avery huffed when she answered.

"You know it's like six in the morning ... and I'm hung over, because I got married yesterday, right?"

"You said you wanted to know if I found her. Well, I did."

Her words took a minute to compute in my alcohol-fogged brain. "What? How? Where?"

I scrambled free of the blankets, shivering in the cool morning air as I realized I wasn't wearing any clothes. I did my best to creep to the dresser and grab clean clothes, struggling into underwear and pants while keeping the phone pressed to my ear.

"I'll send you my location. Come meet me at the Public Garden."

She hung up before I could ask why she was at the Public Garden. I knew I should wake J.T. and let him know what was happening, but he could get a little grumpy in the morning. Still, I had my suspicions that whatever was coming, would be happening mid-day. Noon seemed to be the time to do dark deeds during the light hours of day.

"J.T.," I ruffled his hair and kissed his forehead.

He blinked slowly, opening one eye and then finally the other. "You're dressed. Why are you dressed?"

"I have to go meet Avery. She found Belladonna."

"What?" Confusion made him even cuter and my resolve to go put Desmond's case to bed weakened. My body wanted to crawl back under the covers with him forever. If I stayed here, maybe the world wouldn't be so demanding.

I wanted to tell him I didn't have time to explain, but I was quickly coming to realize that I was running out of time. "Tricia found a partial print on the bullet and it was a match to Adrian. But that isn't possible since he was dead when Desmond was shot. So, it could be Belladonna. Avery managed to find her. I have to go see what she can tell me."

"Could be his dad," J.T. offered through a yawn.

It was a possibility, but his father hadn't been in his son's life for a long while. Belladonna was part of our community and she knew Desmond. "Either way, I need to go find out. I love you."

"I love you, too."

I bent and kissed him on the lips before I remembered Avery was waiting. True to her word, she'd sent me a location on my phone's map app. I texted back, stopping to get coffee—even Saviors need their morning fuel—before driving through the city. Even at this hour I'd expect some traffic on the road, but there were few cars out and about. Maybe the shift in the seasons and the balance of power made people want to hunker down. Even people without magic had to be feeling the effects.

"Why are we in the garden?" I asked when I finally spotted Avery sitting on a bench, her headphones slung around her neck over her scarf like a forgotten pair of earmuffs.

"Because this is where she is." Avery gestured with a gloved hand to a few benches down the way. "She's been here for the last hour."

"How exactly did you find her?" I prodded, taking a long pull from my to-go cup.

"You really don't want to know. But there she is. She's been using some serious power to keep herself under the radar."

"That's not unusual. She was doing that when the Order came after our people three months ago."

"I'm not as sensitive to that sort of thing as you are, but it felt different, like it wasn't just her doing it."

Good to know.

"Did you try and talk to her?"

Avery shook her head. "I kind of got the feeling you'd get pissed at me if I did, especially if it spooked her."

"Fair point." I set my cup down and pulled out my phone. Jacquie wasn't going to be happy about the early morning wake-up call. Although if this meant putting a cold case to bed, she'd have my back.

I didn't bother to check if she responded to my SOS message before I turned back to the bench Avery had been watching. To most it appeared empty, but the few homeless people wandering around avoided it all the same.

"Stay here and wait for Jacquie. I'm going over."

"Please be careful," she called as I abandoned the safety of her bench and marched toward the unknown.

SEVENTEEN

I let the cold air wake me up, heightening my senses as I approached the bench across the way. I could feel the magic pushing me away, urging me to pass by and not stop until I was well away from it. I fought the urge. I felt for the edges of the spell, finding it at the end of the bench. I poured a little of my own will into the equations and unraveled it.

Belladonna appeared before me looking gaunt and disheveled. She was no longer the woman who'd tended my wounds and shown me kindness even when I had been fighting the pull of the Council's guidance and support. Somewhat surprising to me that even after I'd failed to save her son, she'd still treated me with respect. I almost didn't recognize the woman before me now.

"Belladonna?"

Hearing her name made her eyes flutter open. They were vacant, staring like she didn't know me. Her pupils focused on me and after a beat or two, she sat up, starting to move away as far as the back of the bench would allow. "No, you shouldn't be here."

I sat down beside her and took her hands in mine, trying to exude calm even though I had a million questions. I could feel the strangeness of her magic as the spell faded. She'd definitely gotten a boost from somewhere else. "I know you didn't want to be found. But we need to talk. I think you have information that I need."

"What information?" She blinked at me, still struggling to focus.

"About Desmond."

"Desmond? What about him?"

"He's dead. Someone murdered him."

"Oh, oh no, I'm so sorry. But why would I know anything?"

"A fingerprint was found on the bullet and it's a partial match to Adrian."

She scrunched her eyes closed, and she shook her head. "No, that's not right. He wouldn't do that."

"Uh ... He couldn't do that. He's dead, too," I reminded her. She tried to pull free of my grip, but I held tight. "If you're willing, I can go into your mind and get the answers I need without you having to talk."

She chewed her bottom lip so hard I worried she'd draw blood. "Yes. You have my permission."

I inhaled the crisp air through my nose and exhaled through my mouth. My power built up around me. Despite having taken a hit from the charm around my neck on the way over, I could still pick up on the slightest hint of honey at the edges of my magic. That made me smile as I laced my fingers through Belladonna's and went into her mind.

The park vanished and we were standing in a cemetery at a grave marked for Adrian Baptiste. Belladonna stood, holding a simple arrangement of flowers in deep oranges, the color of a summer sunset.

"My sweet boy. I know you had your troubles and you kept me at arm's length. I'm sorry I couldn't be the one you needed. I'm sorry you felt you had to turn to darkness to fulfill that yearning in your heart. Your hands were meant to heal, not harm."

"You can still help me," Adrian's voice was gravelly, but I could still tell it was his.

I turned with the memory of Belladonna to see the teenager standing there in a hoodie. He looked thin and hollow; his face barely recognizable under the scar tissue from the fire.

"You can't be here. You're dead and gone," she argued.

"Our family's business is death, Mom. You know that."

"Your father's side. Not mine. I've always been a healer."

"I guess it just wasn't in me."

"How could you put those girls in danger like that?"

"They weren't supposed to remember anything. And I saved them from death. I promised the Order that they would get what they needed and they swore they'd let them live," he answered as a fit of anger distorted his features.

So, Gabby and Carly's memory blocks had been Adrian's doing. But why had the Order listened to a fifteen-year-old boy? Either Belladonna hadn't wondered the same question or didn't think it was important enough to ask, because she moved on from that topic.

"Why are you here now? How?"

"Because I could feel you grieving, and you needed me. And magic can do some pretty wicked cool stuff."

"They're taking magic. They'll come for me next."

Adrian shook his head. *"They won't. You're safe. I made sure of it. I knew what they'd do, I made them promise they wouldn't touch you."*

Somehow, I doubt he had that much sway over a group of

people hell bent on bringing back dangerous power-hungry monsters.

"I still don't understand how you're standing here." The flowers fell from her hands.

"We live in a world of magic, of impossible things and you can't just accept that a son can be there for his mother when she needs him?"

She stepped closer, reaching out to him and before I could warn her not to, she'd made contact, and everything changed. The memories around us became hazy, almost like she was in a fog, not in control of her actions or her own thoughts. A scene flashed before me as I took in Reuben's magic vanishing into the cloaked figure. Belladonna sat in the corner of the room in silence, just observing the brutal transfer of magic. I could almost taste the hint of his magic on my tongue as the scene skipped ahead again. Other members of the Order flashed by, losing their power as the monster fed, decimating its own followers.

Sunlight flickered around us as Belladonna moved unseeing, loading a sniper rifle with a single shot. Her movements were robotic, so uncharacteristic for her. I watched as she peered through the scope and I walked out of the bank. I didn't want to watch as her finger trembled against the trigger. The sight marked my own chest.

"No, not yet," the death creature rasped as it floated around her.

Its slender fingers wrapped around her hands, holding the trigger until Desmond appeared beside me down below on the street. The scope shifted so she would be firing at him and I could smell the power the creature poured into the bullet. Whether it was to ensure it would find its mark, or be a fatal shot, I didn't care. Maybe it was just trying to mess *with me and confuse my magical senses by using some of Reuben's magic when he was nowhere near the scene. I closed my eyes. I didn't need to watch Desmond die from the sniper's perch.*

I pulled away from Belladonna and as I did so, I could feel the fog lift from around her. She looked at me, clearer eyed than she had since I sat down. "Oh, Ezri, I ... I swear I never meant to hurt anyone."

"It looked like you wanted to take me out," I muttered and repressed a shiver.

I turned just in time to see Jacquie approach the bench. She kept her hands loose at her sides, but I recognized the posture. She was ready for a takedown if necessary.

"You may not have been in total control of your actions, but you accepted that thing's power whether you realized it or not. Believe me, I understand that grief is a powerful motivator. The rules of death are a little hazy for me and my family, too, but you loaded that gun and pulled the trigger. I can't lock up an enigma."

"Want to tell me what's going on, partner?" Jacquie asked. She apparently hadn't been close enough to hear my comment.

"Belladonna and I were having a little trip down memory lane. One that involved the death of our friend, Desmond."

"I see." Jacquie's posture stiffened as she moved to stand on Belladonna's other side.

"I have to take responsibility for what I did," Belladonna stood and held out her hands. "I will not argue or fight. I will make a full confession."

"I don't think we need handcuffs, especially if you're coming willingly. We're just going to drive to the precinct and take your statement. You should get a lawyer," I replied and stood.

I wasn't sure what we were going to say to convince a DA to press charges against her. Maybe we could go with her being angry that I didn't get her son back and Desmond was just collateral in her bid to take out her grief on me.

If Belladonna kept her word and confessed to all of it, even pleading guilty there wouldn't be a need for a trial. However, she still needed counsel to get her the best deal possible. I didn't want her to rot in prison. I'd spent months raging at whoever had taken Desmond from me, but knowing the truth now, all I felt was pity.

We led Belladonna back to my car. I mouthed 'thank you' to Avery as we passed and headed for the precinct. Stepping into the bullpen I half expected people to turn and cheer that I'd solved another case, but no one so much as acknowledged our entry.

"I'll handle the statement. Go fill in the Captain," Jacquie said.

I knocked on the doorframe to the captain's office. "Enter," Captain Beech called, and I nudged the door open enough to slip inside.

"I hear congrats are in order, Trenton," Captain Beech said with a tired smile.

I stared at her in confusion for a minute before realizing she meant the wedding. "Thank you, Ma'am."

"You looking for time off for a honeymoon?"

"Not yet," I answered, twisting the rings around my finger absently. "I actually wanted to let you know that we solved it."

"Solved what?"

"Desmond's case. It turns out the lab missed a partial

print and we traced it to Belladonna Montes. Jacquie's taking her statement now."

I expected Captain Beech to berate me for not leaving the case be. Instead, she looked amused. "I see. And what motive would Ms. Montes have for killing our department's psychologist?"

"Grief does strange things," I answered. "And she may have mentioned that she'd initially been aiming for me." As I stood opposite the woman who'd seen fit to give me a shot by taking me into her precinct as a rookie Detective nine months ago, I wanted to tell her everything. If this death creature got its wish, I had nothing left to lose.

"Well, I suppose you've got the answers you needed. They may not be neat and pretty, but it isn't an open question anymore."

Her tone told me, on some level, she understood that my need to see this case solved carried more behind it than just wanting to get justice for a fallen comrade.

"Captain, I never really thanked you for everything you did for me," I offered unprompted.

"You proved your worth, Detective," she replied. "Now, get out there and do what you were meant to do."

I blinked at her choice of words. "Ma'am ..."

Her smile this time was wider. "You think the people who are counting on you were going to take a chance that you weren't going to end up exactly where they needed you when they needed you?"

I gaped at her. "You've known? This whole time?"

"We weren't going to leave anything to chance," she repeated.

I backed out of the office and tried to wrap my head around the fact that the Authority had made sure I'd been positioned right where they needed me to be to fulfill my destiny. Ezri from nine months ago would have been pissed, railing against the tight grip they were exerting. Despite that, now I realized it wasn't meant to be a bad thing. They were just trying to help me.

EIGHTEEN

Chilled air smacked me in the face the minute I stepped out of the precinct. I couldn't let myself look back at everything I'd worked so hard to achieve. Not when I knew it meant I'd likely never see it again. My destination wasn't far, but I took my time, strolling along Tremont Street and down past Park Street Church. The bells chimed out the hour and I stopped to listen as the sound echoed on the wind. The Common sprawled out across the street ahead of me and I approached it with steady steps. I'd been paying close enough attention to the creature's visits to get the hint that this was where we'd have our final showdown.

The moment my feet touched dead grass and dirty snow piles, I wondered if this sense of peace had settled over my mother the night she sacrificed herself. I'd been ignoring the inevitable as long as possible, but now, I knew what was waiting for me. Also, despite the fact I suspected what was coming, I wasn't afraid. I was sad more than anything else. Sad at the life I wouldn't get to share with J.T. I spun the pair of rings on my left ring finger and let a single tear slip down my cheek. It stung in the cold air, turning icy in seconds.

I'd hated having to say goodbye to J.T., Jacquie, and my dad. I hated having to leave them like this. No matter how much they were part of this journey, it was always going to be me facing off against this monster alone. Except, I wasn't really alone. I pressed my free hand to the pendant resting against my chest. Despite being exposed to the elements, the metal was warm to the touch.

"You are so brave, Ezzie," Grandma's voice said from my left.

I took a few steps farther into the Common. Maybe the world could somehow sense what needed to happen here today, because the space was oddly deserted. At least it meant there was less of a chance for bystanders to get caught in the crossfire. "I don't really have a choice," I finally said softly.

"No, I suppose you don't. Doesn't mean I can't say it. I'm proud of the woman you've become, sweet girl. And I'm here til the bitter end."

I smiled to myself at her promise. "I know you are. I know you all are."

I felt a hand slide into my right, and I turned to see Desmond standing there beside me, tears in his eyes. "I fucking hate you," I said, fighting back tears of my own.

"I'm sorry it took so long for me to come out and play," he whispered.

Out of the corner of my eye, I watched Grandma disappear. This was a private moment between Des and me. I knew he wasn't really here, but I threw my arms around him anyway, holding him tight. "I figured it out. I solved the case."

"I know." He squeezed me tight. "I never doubted you would."

"I'm sorry I couldn't save you," I wiped at my eyes, knowing I looked crazy.

"I know that, too. But let's just say the trip to Ireland wasn't just eye-opening for you. While you were communing with ancestors, I was getting a glimpse at the future. I don't know if J.T. got the same treatment, but whatever magic Aoife invoked made it crystal clear that my days were numbered."

"No, that can't be right. She said I had to pay her debt. That I was the one who was supposed to set things right again."

"And you will. You're the last living member of Harrow's blood," he pointed out and started walking toward the center of the Common.

I picked up the pace to keep up with his longer strides. "Why would that mean you had to die?"

"Think about the prophecy, Ez. The wording," he prompted. His tone carried a hint of exasperation.

"I know the damn wording," I grumbled, but it dawned on me after a pace or two. "Damn it. I should have realized it sooner." Unlike Eleanor's prophecy centuries ago that specified the gender of the world's Savior, Neveah's prophecy was more gender neutral. But it was clear that the last of Harrow's blood was involved. Like it or not, Desmond and I both were of Harrow's blood. Which meant only one of us could walk into this fight alive.

"You should have told me." I punched him in the arm.

"If I had, you'd have tried to save me, and we could be having a very different conversation right now."

Did he know how close we'd come to that reality? If

Belladonna had managed to shoot me, he'd be the one facing Death's child instead.

"We both know that no matter how much I had wanted to be the Savior, I wasn't the one the world chose," Des continued. It had led to drama between our families. Not enough to never speak again, but he'd told me more than once he wished he could take the burden from me. "It had to be you. So, that meant the bullet had to be for me."

"You really have a bad habit of keeping stuff to yourself when I might actually benefit from knowing it," I said and stopped in the middle of the path.

"I knew if I gave you all the answers, you'd try to fight your destiny."

"All the answers? You could have at least given me a little hint," I griped.

"Not to break up the party, but do you feel that?" Grandma interrupted.

I closed my eyes and focused on the world around me. The sun may have been shining, but I could sense the darkness closing in. It called to me, wrapping tight around the pit of my stomach, drawing me onward. Garlic tickled my nose as the spell woke up again. Taggart's magic wriggled within me, trying to turn my magic against me with every step. Spearmint beat back the foul taste in my mouth as Desmond lent me some of his precious reserve to keep the darkness within at bay for just a little longer.

I followed the path to the center of the Common. *Of course, it ends here.* The site of my first real clash with the Order would be the place it all came to a head. I expected the cloaked figure who'd been invading my mind for months to be just a figment of my imagination at this point, but there it stood, wrapped in a hooded cloak. From this distance it looked short. Maybe my perspective had always been off in our mental clashes, but I could have sworn it was taller. I sensed more than saw Grandma and Desmond disappear back into the heart of the pendant.

"So, do we just like beat the shit out of each other until one of us yields or what?" I called. I could almost hear Desmond in the back of my mind chastising me for being a mouthy idiot.

"I do not need to lay hands on you, Savior, to end you," the figure replied.

I caught a hint of a familiar voice underneath the rasp, but I couldn't place it. I took a few steps forward and the figure mirrored me until we were within an arm's length of one another. A bone chilling gust of wind whipped between us, pulling the hood of the cloak away to reveal a dark-skinned figure, its features disfigured by burns.

Oh, shit. Adrian.

"You're Death's child," I croaked, my words coming out more as a statement than question.

He nodded his head. "I gave my body over to it, making me stronger than I ever could have been in life."

It made sense now. He had in fact been there in the cemetery that day when he approached Belladonna. He'd used stolen magic and likely some of his own family's power to control her. I knew there wasn't anything I could say to him to make him realize what he'd done. I doubted he'd even been in control of himself after the monster took hold. "I'm sorry."

"Sorry? Why?" He scoffed, his voice tight as if he was still fighting smoke inhalation.

"You were just a kid. You were lonely and you wanted to know your family. The Order took advantage of that, twisted things to make you believe that they could give you power."

"You're wrong. I went to them willingly," he said, puffing out his chest. No matter how tough he was trying to be, he still moved in the body of a badly burned teenage boy and his chest strained against the action.

"What did you do to get them to let the girls go? To leave your mother's magic untouched?"

His confidence faltered. "They needed a willing vessel. I offered it to them."

"But, why?"

"They said I would learn all about my power over death. And I have. I even made sure the girls weren't hurt." He pounded a clawed hand against the cloak. "I did that ... Me."

"Adrian, they may not have physically hurt them, but their minds haven't healed. Not entirely. You caused so much pain and for what? The promise of having control over death?"

"You grew up knowing you were special. But what was I? No one. Just some kid from Southie. Now, I have power. All of it. And I'm going to have yours, too."

I caught the myriad of scents swirling around him. I picked up on Reuben's vinegar and even Janty's nauseating scent among them. This creature had turned its tactics against the Order, growing so power-hungry that it destroyed its own acolytes.

"So, say you're right and you take me out. Then what?"

He laughed. "Why would I tell you?"

I gestured around at the empty space. "Who am I going to tell? Besides, in this scenario you've taken me off the playing board. Not like I'm in a position to blab the plan. So, what, world domination?"

"The time of darkness will reign, and magic will be wielded as it was meant to."

"Except, if you keep taking people out, there will be no one left to use it and you'll be reigning over no one. I saw Belladonna's memories. I know you've basically wiped out most of the Order's members already," I pointed out.

"You're stalling," he scoffed.

"Damn right I am," I admitted. "But you can't blame a girl for trying."

For all of my self-realization and acceptance on the walk here, now that I was facing down this monster, I didn't want to take the last step off the proverbial cliff. He didn't give me a chance to acclimate before a literal pulsing wave of magic shot out and knocked me backward. I landed hard on my back and I groaned when my head hit the ground with a 'crack.' Black spots danced in my vision for a few seconds before the nausea hit me. Fighting back the urge to vomit, I climbed to my feet.

I felt the world's magic crackling around me like the beginning of a lightning storm. It may be the Winter Solstice, but the world still needed me to make this sacrifice. Even if this thing wanted hell on earth, the rest of reality wanted to maintain balance, which meant it was rooting for me. I let the magic pour through me, charging up my own power. It fed the kernel of dark magic within me and I was finally going to let it out to play. After all, Taggart had reminded me that dark magic was stronger today.

I pulled Taggart's spell from the center of my body, willing it to liquify and pool in my hands. Adrian wanted dark magic; he was about to get some. I watched as the magic took on form, swirling and molding itself into a glowing grey mass like the stone it had once been. The smell of chlorine popped around me as the world lent me what magic it could. The tips of my fingers and my palms tingled with the spell.

Stop this thing in its tracks.

Lobbing it overhand like a baseball, I sent the spell hurtling toward the thing that used to be Adrian. The sphere collided with the creature and it staggered back a couple steps. I kept myself in check—no reason to cheer just yet—as I watched the spell spread outward, turning the creature to stone.

It lifted its head and laughed; a bone-chilling sound. "You didn't think that through, did you Savior? Today of all days, you think darkness will stop me?"

The stone receded, turning liquid again and melted into the creature's slender clawed hands. It shimmered, turning to fire and I went sailing backward again, my hair smelling singed. It had been a Hail Mary. If I was being honest with myself, I'd really just wanted to find a way to get it out of me and break the bond I had never intended to create.

My left side ached as I tried to stand and breathe in. I pressed my hand to my ribcage and could feel something shift. Wonderful. I almost regretted not bringing J.T. along to help with injuries, but I knew I couldn't put him in the line of fire. None of the people I loved could be here.

I didn't have time to eke out any of my own magic to ease the pain before a tidal wave of dark magic, smelling of so many scents my nose could no longer distinguish individual ones, hit me. I managed to stay on my feet, but I was now a good ten feet away from the creature.

"You must use all power at your disposal," Aoife's voice said from beside me.

I felt heat warm my fingers and my side. The pain lessened and while I was grateful not to have a broken rib anymore, I wanted to scold her for using up what little magic she'd left in the pendant.

"I have plenty enough for that," she said, as if reading my mind.

Of course, she did. She's part of me. Every person left who gave some of their magic is here within me, in the pendant. "This thing is kicking my ass," I ground out.

"That's what you get for trying to use dark magic," Grandma noted, tilting her aviators down to give me side eye.

"You are incredibly strong, Ez. You were literally born to fight this monster," Desmond said and squeezed my right hand.

He was right. I reached deep down into my own power, pulling it up from my core. I let it ripple over my skin like armor made of the ripest strawberries, tinged with the barest hint of honey. Even if he couldn't be here with me in person, J.T. was still with me. Putting my intent out into the world was easy. I needed to protect this world and there was no purer intent out there.

The Common around me came into sharper focus as my senses zeroed in on the creature waiting for me. "I'd say you're right, but you really don't need the ego stroke," I called out to it. "Besides, I don't really care what you do with that spell. It just means it's not there anymore trying to fight my own power."

I got a running start and it was like space just shrunk. One moment we were several feet apart and then, my fist slammed into his face, sending him staggering backward. Ribbons of magic, swirling with bright red and orange light zipped out from my hands, binding its wrists together.

He struggled and I was about to offer up a quip about struggling making them tighter when the bonds broke. "You just don't get it yet, Savior. You cannot beat me." It didn't bother using magic this time when it backhanded me.

I tasted blood as I went stumbling sideways into a tree trunk. Neveah's words whispered in the back of my mind. *The last of Harrow's blood must flow forevermore.* I was the last of Harrow's blood now, but I carried an entire lineage with me, waiting to be unleashed. Wait, maybe the blood wasn't literal. Magic lives in every part of us, including our blood.

It was time. No more avoiding the inevitable.

J.T.'s smiling face flashed before me along with Jacquie's laughter filling my ears. The ghost of my dad's fiercest hug wrapped around me, reminding me of everything I was about to lose and I couldn't help but shed a few tears. I pushed myself away from the tree and wiped the tears I felt staining my cheeks. I wasn't going to face death crying. I clasped the pendant in my right hand and felt the pink stone warm at its center. One by one, the remnants of my ancestor's magic poured out around me, taking form until I was surrounded by dozens of people. Grandma and Desmond stood on either side of me. I caught Theodora and Aoife among the ranks behind me. The floral fragrances of heather and jasmine mixed with the earthy scents of wheat and moss.

"You're right. I can't beat you with only my magic. But that's the thing you don't seem to understand. I don't just have my own magic. I am a vessel for my entire bloodline. You may have taken other people's power, but each and every person in my bloodline gave a piece of themselves for this very moment. And that sort of sacrifice is so much more powerful than you are or ever will be."

One by one I felt my family, who had given freely of their magic melt into my own power until their scents were indistinguishable from my own. The power built up around me, but it didn't harden into armor or any sort of defense.

Instead, it pooled in my core, building until I could feel it ready to burst.

I expected the feeling to make it difficult to breathe. Watching Adrian try to wield so much power had looked painful, but there was no pain, no sense of constriction. If anything, I felt lighter, freer.

The world fell away and all that remained were the creature and me. It came charging at me, but I was ready. Ready for all of this to end. I held my arms out at my sides and let the magic flow through me and out into the world with the simple intent to *protect*.

The creature collided with the outpouring of power. Ever so slowly, my magic coiled around its form, binding tight until it looked like a strawberry-wrapped mummy. The magic squeezed tighter and with a sudden 'pop,' the creature turned to dust and ash, carried away on the wind. With a pulse, all of the remaining magic fled my body, blanketing the city and the world beyond. My knees buckled and the edges of my vision began to darken. My breathing came in slow rasps as the wind tugged at my hair. I clung to the sounds of the city for just a little longer, chasing the rumble of the trains and cars speeding past.

I felt the vibration of the footsteps more than heard them as J.T.'s face appeared above me. How had he found me? I wanted to smile up at him, but I'd lost control of my body. It felt almost as if I were floating, barely tethered to this world anymore.

"Stay with me," J.T. said.

I wanted to stay, so badly it hurt. Only it wasn't how the world worked. I didn't always get what I wanted. The Savior didn't always get to go home at the end of the day. I watched as he did chest compressions and the sense of floating vanished as it started to pull me back in. However, no matter how much I wanted to cling to the world, death was inevitable. More than that, it was necessary. So many members of my family had sacrificed themselves, to get me here. One more sacrifice was needed to set the balance of the world to right. I was the last of Harrow's blood and I was willing to pay that price.

Soon, J.T.'s face faded to nothing.

DECEMBER 31, 2017

EPILOGUE

The sun sat low in the sky, already on its afternoon descent. The cemetery is quiet, peaceful. The city would be alive with parties and fireworks in just a few short hours as a new year rolled in. The ground was firm and hard, but clearly disturbed in a small plot located on the back row. There's no headstone yet, but there will be soon. Footfalls crunched against the cold ground as J.T. appeared, his hood pulled up against the harsh winter air.

I wished I could feel that biting chill just one more time, but I was beyond the sensations of hot and cold now. I couldn't help watching him as he bent down and brushed some stray earth back into place. His body obscured my view so I couldn't tell what he was doing. When he finally stood up, I could see he'd placed the pentacle in the dirt, covering it over so it wouldn't get swept away with the wind.

"Hey, Ez. I know you probably can't hear me ... but maybe you can. It's been a week and it still doesn't feel real, that you're gone."

I moved closer to him, longing to wrap him in a hug.

Through everything we'd been through, he'd been a pillar holding me up; even when I didn't realize he was doing it in the years we spent apart. And now we'd be apart again for a very long time. He wiped tears from his eyes with the back of his gloved hand.

"God, I miss you." He rubbed the top of his left hand and I could spot the slight bulge of the ring on his finger. "We didn't have enough time." His breath caught in his throat. "I'm not blaming anyone," he added quickly. Like he was going to offend me.

"I know we didn't have enough time together," I whispered.

He laughed and gave a sad smile. "You know, it's almost like I can still feel you around me, keeping an eye on me."

I stepped back as his words settled over me. He wasn't wrong. I hadn't been able to move on yet. The people I loved were holding me tight to this world, no matter how hard J.T. had tried to keep me alive in it. As I shuffled back, I felt a hand reach for mine. I didn't think anything of it, letting whoever it was give me support. I turned to find my mother standing there as she'd been nine months ago when she'd given up the rest of her magic for me.

"How is this possible?" At least I think the words came out of my mouth.

"We're in the same place now, sweetheart. I'm so sorry it had to come to this. I never wanted this for you."

"The world didn't give me a choice. I had to pay the debt Aoife owed to keep the balance. To set it right."

She gave my hand a squeeze. "I know. But I wanted you to have a full life with all the happiness you deserved."

I looked at J.T. as he stood there, blowing into his hands and shifting from foot to foot to keep warm. "I was happy. But I knew it was only a matter of time until this came along. I wish I could just give him one more goodbye. I didn't exactly say it before all of this. Not the way I should have."

"I feel that way all the time," Desmond's voice rang out from my right.

"I'm still mad at you," I reminded him, nudging his shoulder.

"I know and I'm sorry I didn't tell you what I'd seen. But look at it this way, we both get to hang out together for eternity or whatever is waiting for us next."

The thought of spending the rest of my afterlife, or whatever this was, with my family who'd given up their lives for me wasn't such a bad consolation prize. Desmond wrapped his arm around my shoulders just as another set of footsteps crunched on the ground. J.T. turned and wiped at his face again.

"I hope I'm not disturbing you," Dad said, a small wreath in his hand.

"No. I could use the company, honestly," he answered and took a step to his left so they could both stand at my grave.

Dad set the wreath on top of the pentacle, keeping it more firmly in place. Dad fiddled with his hat. I knew he wanted to say something, but maybe was too ashamed or scared to voice it.

"Do you still feel her?" Dad finally voiced.

J.T. nodded. "Everywhere. It's the grief, right? I'm still in the denial phase?"

"I don't know. With all this magic stuff, isn't it possible that some part of her is still here? I mean, if the rest of the family could put themselves in that pendant, couldn't she?"

"I tried to sense any magic in it, and I couldn't," Avery's voice interjected into the conversation.

Dad and J.T. both turn to see her carrying flowers. She stopped three graves down at Desmond's and placed them against the headstone. She pulled a few buds free and laid them on mine across Dad's wreath making a pentacle.

"What do you mean?" Dad choked out.

"I tried to see if there was any magical signature on it and there's nothing. It may have been super powerful at one point, but it's just a necklace now. The power's gone."

"You know, I'm not saying I'm jealous or anything," Desmond leaned in to whisper in my ear even though the living couldn't hear our conversation, "but you didn't have to show me up by dying the way you did."

"Okay, first of all, that shit hurt. A lot. And second, you are totally jealous," I quipped.

Back at the gravesite, Avery stepped around to be on J.T.'s other side, taking his hand in hers. "I think I feel Desmond sometimes still, like he's watching over me. The world's magic is connected, and it never really ends. Like Ezri said, it just takes up root in someone new. So, yeah, maybe they are out there somewhere and maybe one day if we're lucky we'll cross paths with their magic again. Even if it's in someone new. Maybe we'll get to teach them to use their powers."

J.T.'s shoulders shook with emotion and I could hear him sniffling at her words. I was dead and even I got teary at the thought. Somehow, I knew that my magic wouldn't be taking up residence in anyone new. Not for a long time anyway. My last act had been to protect everyone in this city.

"I wish I could say goodbye, just one more time," I sighed.

"You're the Savior, I'm pretty sure if anyone can communicate beyond the grave, it's you," Desmond replied.

"He's right. Besides, you're connected to this place. You are literally laid to rest here," Mom added.

"Yeah, because that's not creepy," I muttered. I understood what she meant, though. The cemetery made me feel more real than I had since dying. I watched my loved ones share in their grief and I couldn't just stand by any longer.

"Here goes nothing," I said and for what was probably the last time. I felt my magic build up around me, fortifying me with the heady scent of ripe strawberries fresh from the field, drizzled with the little bit of J.T.'s magic that had become a part of me during our wedding ceremony. My form took on mass and while my heart didn't quite beat again, it was the closest I was going to feel to alive ever again.

Without thinking I extended the spell, feeding the temporary step back into the mortal realm to my Mom and Desmond. Giving them a final goodbye, too. The trio at my grave seemed unaffected by the spell taking shape behind them until J.T. sniffed again, looking left and right.

"Do you smell strawberries?" The hint of hope and longing in his tone nearly broke me.

I didn't want to freak them out by just throwing myself at him. I let them come to the realization that something magical was happening. Avery tilted her head to one side and nodded.

"It's like someone dumped an entire bushel. It's not a smell you should find at a cemetery, not in the dead of winter."

Mom nudged me forward and I stumbled on some frozen dirt. It was enough to draw their attention. One by one they turned around to face me.

"Uh, hey guys. Surprise!" *God, I could be such a dork.*

To think there was a time I wouldn't have spoken to them at all, let alone joke with them.

"This isn't real," Dad gasped, clutching at his chest.

"It's real, Dad," I told him and reached out to take his gloved hand.

"I ... How?" His fingers shook against mine.

"Magic, of course," Mom answered and stepped up beside me.

"You said she was gone," he rambled.

"That piece of me was gone, but our daughter is far more powerful than any of us. She did this. She gave us this last chance at a proper goodbye."

"Hey there, cinnamon," Desmond said to Avery as she stared at him, open mouthed.

She gave a hiccup of laughter and threw her arms around his neck. "I hate you for not saying goodbye, you jerk. But also, I love you. And I miss you."

"I love you, too," he said just loud enough for me to hear.

"I don't know how much you all talk in the afterlife or whatever this is, but we got you justice," she added.

He cupped her face and kissed her nose. "I was there with her the whole time. I saw what she did and how you helped. I'm glad you didn't lose yourself on my account. I don't think I could have handled it."

"I've updated my playlist," she said and dragged him along the headstones to his grave.

I turned to face J.T. as he still stood by the spot where my headstone would go. Tears stained his cheeks and unshed ones glittered in his eyes. I took his hand and led him to a nearby bench.

"You feel so ... alive," he whispered and wiped at his face.

"Small bonus of being dead, winter is done kicking my ass," I commented.

"I miss you. More than I ever thought was possible given everything we've been through."

"If dying hadn't done me in, leaving you behind when we just started to explore our future together would have killed me," I told him.

"I think I understand what you felt when you lost your mom now. That sense of helplessness and loss of purpose—feeling rudderless."

"Unlike me, you know what happened. I know you were there at the end. I know you tried to save me. I could feel you, but I had to go. For this to be over, for you to be safe, I had to let go. You don't have to wonder or listen to people make up shit that's not true."

"I don't fully understand what happened, but I guess none of us ever really will."

"The details are a little hazy for me, too. But the creature Bearach created all those centuries ago finally got its chance to do some damage and my life was the price that had to be paid to keep it from winning."

"Is it wrong I kind of hate Aoife for forcing you into that position?"

"No. But, without her and the decision she made, I wouldn't have existed at all. So, double-edged sword and everything."

He nodded and a small half-smile crept onto his lips. "Good point."

"Tell Jacque I miss her and that I hope she isn't too hard on whatever new partner Captain Beech gives her."

"I don't think her new partner is going to have any trouble handling her. She's transferring to the FBI, working with Agent Cartwright."

"Bad guys beware," I replied. The change seemed abrupt, but I could understand her need of something new. Losing your partner isn't something you get over easily or quickly. Besides, maybe she'd reconsidered Molly's suggestion to do undercover work.

"So, I'm guessing this isn't going to be a recurring thing," J.T. sighed and gripped my hand tight in his.

As if on cue, the world around me flickered, growing dim around me for a few seconds. I felt less tethered to this plane and the man I'd married. I squeezed my eyes shut and sent up a silent plea. *Just a little more time. You owe me that much.*

"I wish I could stay longer, but I think I may have overstayed my welcome," I answered when the world came back into focus. I couldn't tell if the blip in being solid had been noticeable to Desmond or Mom.

"Magic owes you so much," he sighed.

I kissed his lips. "I know. And I'm not going to be far from you, even if we can't talk like this again. My last spell before I died was to protect my city. It's like I'm a part of everything. It's hard to put into words or even assign a feeling to it. Only I'll be around. Plus, every time you do a spell, I'll be there."

He hung his head. "So, no passing your magic onto someone else somewhere down the line?"

I shrugged. "Never say never, but not any time soon. I think maybe the world reclaimed my power, because that's where it belonged."

"And that thing you fought. What happened to it?"

"All of that magic is out there, looking for new hosts. So, don't be surprised if you see a spike in magical bloodlines surfacing in a few years. Try to get them in on the side of good." Although, as I'd learned over the last nine months, good can't exist without evil. There was always a balance that had to be maintained. Maybe we'd learned our lesson now and the world would stay balanced for a while on its own.

The world flickered again, and I held tighter to J.T.'s hand. He kissed my knuckles and pointed to where my parents stood over by Mom's grave. "Go say goodbye to your dad."

"I'm not ready to leave you," I admitted.

"I'm not ready, either, but your dad deserves some closure, too."

He gave me a little shove forward, and I staggered over my own grave. If I could still feel the cold, I would have shivered at the weirdness of it alone. Dad looked less shaken now as I approached. He pulled Mom and I into a three-way hug. He didn't speak, but it was enough to tell me how much he loved and missed me and Mom. The fact we'd never get to have a hug like this again overwhelmed me, bringing tears to my eyes.

"I didn't think the dead could cry," I sniffled and pressed the palms of my hands into my face.

"Love is a powerful emotion. It can bring all sorts of other things to the surface," Mom said as Dad reached for my hand.

"Tell me one thing. Are you at peace? Truly?" His words drew J.T., Avery, and Desmond's attention.

"I am," I answered, standing tall and looking him in the face. I'd accepted the fact that I had to die for the world to finally be safe. I could feel the balance had been restored and knew the people I loved would look after each other.

I never expected to die at age twenty-five or to have saved the world so many times. Magic had asked the ultimate price of me and I'd paid it, because I was the Savior. I was born for this very fate. Dad's fingers slipped through my hand as it went translucent and immaterial. Mom and Desmond shimmered around me once again.

"I love you all. I know it took me a long time to remember what was important, but all of you helped get me to pull my head out of my ass and own my destiny. Look after each other."

Behind Dad, a blinding light appeared, and my feet moved of their own volition. Mom and Desmond appeared beside me, each taking one of my hands in theirs.

"So, I guess the whole going into the light thing is real," I murmured as the three of us together stepped through to face whatever adventure waited for us beyond death.

The End...?

QUICK AUTHOR'S NOTE

IF THERE'S one thing I'm not afraid to do, it's kill characters. Even if that means my main protagonists. But, then again, I have felt like this was the natural trajectory for Ezri's story all along. And in a manner of speaking, she gets a happy ending being with her mom and Des again.

I am normally a very linear writer. I don't jump around from point A to point M and back to point B. But for this book, I got a very short way into the start of the book and I went and wrote the epilogue. I think part of me needed to know that Ezri and everyone else was going to be okay in the end so that I could write the rest of the story. Then, I wrote the final battle chapter (or at least the first draft of it) so that I could get through her death scene.

Knowing that this was the end of Ezri's journey was bittersweet. I loved creating the magical world that she inhabited and I grew attached to many of the side characters. Which is why the *Seasons of Magic* 'verse is expanding!

I needed a little time away from the world (so I went and wrote some other books) but I'm back now and picking up a couple years down the line following Kayla, Jacquie and FBI Molly (as my lovely beta reader Molly calls her). There were still pieces of their stories I wanted to explore and so a spin-off series seemed like the perfect way to do it!

Turn the page to see a sneak peek at the first book in the *Agents of Magic* series...

ABOUT THE AUTHOR

Sarah Biglow is a *USA Today* bestselling author. She lives in Massachusetts with her husband and son. She is a licensed attorney and spends her days combatting employment discrimination as an Investigator with the Massachusetts Commission Against Discrimination.

You can find an up-to-date list of all my books here